I

AM

THE

SWARM

I
AM
THE
SWARM

HAYLEY CHEWINS

VIKING

FOR LIALE —H.C.

VIKING
An imprint of Penguin Random House LLC
1745 Broadway, New York, New York 10019

First published in the United States of America by Viking,
an imprint of Penguin Random House LLC, 2025

Visit us online at PenguinRandomHouse.com.

Library of Congress Cataloging-in-Publication Data is available.

ISBN 9780593623862

1 3 5 7 9 10 8 6 4 2

Printed in the United States of America

BVG

Edited by Meriam Metoui | Design by Sophie Erb

Text set in Venetian301 BT

CONTENT WARNINGS

I Am the Swarm portrays characters dealing with depression, self-harm, disordered eating, sexual harassment, and dysfunctional family dynamics. It refers to attempted suicide and contains graphic descriptions of blood.

I have got to make everything that has happened to me good for me.

—**Oscar Wilde**, *De Profundis*

PART ONE

SEVENTEEN DAYS BEFORE THE WASPS

I get my magic on a Saturday.

Three days after I turn fifteen.

Like it nearly forgot about me.

Like I almost got free.

My fifteenth birthday arrives quietly,

like someone
opening a window
in a house
down the street.

I keep watching for the magic.

Watch myself from the inside. Find nothing.

In the afternoon,
Ouma comes over for tea,
her Yorkie, Hildegarde,
tucked under her arm.

The magic is already hours late,
and no one is mentioning that it's late,
not Ouma, who sits down
and immediately starts feeding a lemon cream
to Hildegarde, and not Mamma,
who is cutting chocolate cake,
sucking icing off her finger.

We sit in the cool dining room,
the three of us, and the fact that Mora isn't there
makes the house feel like one big echo.
The table is too wide. The chairs are too far apart.

Then Mamma's phone rings.

Mamma is twenty-nine today,
wearing bright-green heels
and dangly earrings. Thin as an actress.

She comes back. Still holding the knife.
"Sorry, baby, I have to go." She doesn't explain.
Doesn't say, "Your sister needs me."
If she said it. If she actually said the words.
I would be able to ask questions.

I would be able to say:

"Do you really think   that I don't need you?"

Ouma and I,
we listen to Mamma
gathering her things.

Walking around,
whispering
that she can't find her keys.
Until the door slams.

When Mamma's gone,
Ouma says,
"Has everything been
all right at home, Nell?"

Ouma's English is formal,
slowly and carefully pronounced.
Her accent is like cream
floating on the surface of her words,
making all the consonants softer.

"Things have been okay."
"She's twenty-eight now?"
"Twenty-nine."

I've been watching
Mamma change for so long
that I always know.

Ouma nods. "That's better. That's—"
"She's been sixteen a lot, though."
"I suppose it's understandable."
I cut myself a piece of cake. "She forgot to make the tea."
"Nell," says Ouma.
"Your mamma.
She's trying very hard."

Mamma's magic:

her age is always changing.

She's never younger than fifteen, the age the magic found her.
And she's never older than her actual age.

In between fifteen and forty-two,
there is a staircase.

The steps
are all
different heights.
You can't walk up or down
without tripping.

Ouma watches me
make two cups of tea,
but I can see
her mind is elsewhere.

I can see
she's thinking about
Mora's empty room.

Long after Ouma goes home,
I hear Mamma's car singing up the road.

"How was she?" I ask
when she steps through the door.

"Nell, I can't talk now."

In the light of the entrance, she's younger,
leaning against the doorframe as she kicks off her shoes.

She's fifteen.

She has been
fifteen
too many times to count.

I will only ever turn fifteen once.

Go to my room. Sit at the piano.
But my fingers won't move.
Even before I've started to play.
I've already given up.

I lie on my bed and I think about the magic.
About how it's going to come. How I can't stop it.

All the women in my family have some kind of magic.
It's the kind that goes crooked through you,
growing at a slant, like trees bowing to the icy Atlantic wind
that shrieks over Cape Town.

Ouma says it's always been this way.
Her mother, her mother's mother.
The magic is passed down the line,
a cursed family heirloom that nobody wants.

I've never wanted it. But that has never mattered.
No matter what I want. I'm still going to get it.

I can't say this to anyone, though.

I never talk to Dad
about magic,
and Ouma is gone now,
and Mamma is fifteen tonight,
doesn't want to talk.

One daughter's magic
is already too much to carry.

The next evening, we visit Mora at the clinic,
even though Mamma is so young she could be Mora's twin.

Dad never comes with us.

Somehow,
every time we plan on going,
he manages to have a phone call that can't wait.
Meeting. Crisis. Unhappy client.

Tonight, he's pacing up and down the pathway that leads to the garage,
his phone lighting the side of his face. Half shadow. Half ghost.

We brush past him, but he doesn't notice.

Mamma stops on the path
and watches him
not seeing her.

She squeezes his arm softly to say goodbye,
so she doesn't interrupt his conversation.

She's sixteen,
and Dad is his unchanging forty-four,
and she looks small beside him,
and her eyes speak quietly
about all the things she wants to ask for
but can't mention.

He raises his eyebrows. She raises her eyebrows back.

Then she walks to the car, and I follow her.

I never try to talk to Dad when he's on the phone.

I already know. He's unreachable.

We sit in the visitors' room,
waiting for Mora to appear.

Then she's there,
in the narrow doorway,
her sleeves tugged down
over her hands,
her hair greasy at the roots.

"Mori," Mamma says, patting the chair beside her,
but Mora leaves space between them.

I can see Mamma is trying not to look hurt,
but when she's this young
everything shows up on her face
like light reflecting off still water.

"How's it going?" Mamma asks,
reaching for Mora across the empty space, not touching her.

Mora shrugs. She shoves her sleeves up
and I see the scars that have Jackson Pollocked her forearms.
I know they go all the way up to her shoulders,
slipping across her collarbones. Some of the scars are thick as fingers,
shiny as fish scales. There are fresh scabs, too, reddish, rough as gravel.
"Why do you keep coming?" she barks.
And it takes me a second to realize she's talking to me.
"Nell," she says. "What are you doing here?"

"She's your sister," says Mamma.

"I don't want her here," says Mora.

"Mora—"

"I don't want her here."

That's when Mora starts to scream.

She leans forwards in her chair and screams in my face,

scratching at her scarred arms.

A line of blood

trickles down towards her right wrist,

and I can hear it.

It's soft, but it's still there:

the music trapped inside.

Right there, in the waiting room,

delicate harmonies waver,

humming like a hall of old fridges.

"I think we should go," says Mamma.

Looks at me. Like I did something wrong.

Mora got her magic
the second she turned fifteen
because that's what she's like:

everything is drawn to her quicker.

She was fifteen.
I was almost fourteen.
The first time I heard it.

She was sitting in the dripping garden,
cross-legged on the orange bricks,
the last of October's rain darkening the grout,
deepening the color of the grass.

It was chilly. She shivered as she said,
"Nell. Listen to this."

She cut into her clean white forearm with a razor blade,
a silver thing turning light into violence.

"Listen," she said again.

There was music coming out of the cut.
Bright music. The reddest I had ever heard.
I put my ear close to the wound.
It crept into me. That red music.
It sat, pooling, in my stomach.

I stood up. Backed away.

At arm's length, I watched the blood spill out of her.

Red is a girl's color. Red nail polish. Roses.
Lipstick and red every month. So I shouldn't have been shocked to see it.
But it was a color and a sound together, like my sister's body was a speaker.

There was the blood: sparkling out of the cut.
And there was the music. As she bled, it got louder.

"It's in my blood." She laughed like she couldn't believe it.
"It's in there. Nell. You can hear it, right?"

My mouth was too dry to speak but I nodded.

I could hear it. Then.

I still hear it now.

Mora made me swear not to tell Mamma.

I swore on the piano. I swore on the mountain
we could see from the edge of the garden,
shaped like an elephant, a dark cave for an eye.
I swore on the cherries picked from the trees,
their sour taste like poison. I swore on every flower.

I swore on the unchanging cold of the ocean,
wild foam licking at wet-black rock.

I would do it. Of course I would do it. I did everything she told me then.

The weeks went on. Months.
Wet spring morphed into crackling summer.

Despite the heat, Mora covered the cuts with long sleeves.
Mamma and Dad hardly noticed.

More and more time in her room. Music rattling the closed door.

There was no wind anymore. Only hot, still air.

I didn't say
a thing.

But after a while,
the secret
was heavy
as handfuls
of wet sand.

In the end.

I had to tell.

Mora has hated me

ever since.

When my magic arrives,
Mora isn't there to see it.
It happens without her knowing.
It happens to me alone.

It comes when I'm sitting at the piano,

trying to figure out a new song.

Fiddling, fingers fidgeting, semitoning up and down,

letting myself be the knot that music is made of,

and it comes, the phrase I'm looking for—

out of my mouth and the ends of my fingers at the same time.

It's like a wave pushing through me, like I am the wave, bending.

Right there, on the piano's keys, yellow ladybugs appear.

I count them over and over, five ladybugs, each tiny as a pinkie's nail,

and if I wasn't fifteen and I wasn't expecting it,

wasn't expecting the magic, I'd think I was dreaming.

But I am fifteen and I am a Strand girl and I know it's the magic,

my magic. I blink at them. Their purring wings.

My heart: a pocket of light. But then they lift into the air,

float, fall across the floor like wind-carried seeds,

and somewhere inside me a door has closed.

And I hope for that bright feeling to come back. But it doesn't.

I walk through the house, looking for Mamma,
cupping one of the ladybugs in my hand.
I want to tell her that my magic has come.

I don't have words for it yet,
but I can show her.
I can show her the ladybug.
I can try to explain.

I find her upstairs, in the en suite bathroom,
staring at her face in the mirror, a hand on her cheek.

"Mamma—"

"I look exactly like her. All week, it's been like this."

She turns to face me. I close my hand over the dead ladybug.

Mamma is sixteen again today. She looks so much like Mora.

"It's my fault she's in that place."

"It's not your fault, Mamma."

"Not my fault? Whose fault is it, then?"

"It's the magic's fault," I tell her, trying to sound like I believe it.

Mamma's mouth
is a bruise
of purple lipstick.

"Exactly," she says.

"What do you mean?"

"Who do you think she got it from? Dad?"

Her laugh stings like wind on the beach.

It takes a while for the ladybugs to come back.

When they come back. They are not ladybugs.

This is how it happens.

Mamma's trying to make it up to me:

missing my birthday,
not even asking about the magic.

She hates the beach
but she loves Kirstenbosch—
manicured green
mossing up the side of Table Mountain,
beds of strelitzias,
gangs of spiked aloe,
proteas as big as ostrich eggs.

So we go there,
where the summer is most summery.
Green and hot, ocean wind called off,
turned back to the Antarctic,
leaving us stranded and sweating.

We're walking up a winding path.
The trees reach for each other over our heads.

I'm trying to tell Mamma about a book I've been reading.

It's a small thing like that. Just trying to tell her about a book.
"Half of it is narrated by a cat.
And the main character, he's—"

I stop talking.

She isn't looking at me.
I can see she's not listening.
She's staring at the shallow stream dancing past us,
light sparkling on ruddy water.

She's a little older than Mora today. Seventeen and she
hasn't stopped frowning. That's why
I'm telling her about the book. To distract her,
make her feel better. But it isn't working.
She tugs at her eyelashes with pinched fingertips.

This is the moment that gets the magic out of me.

A cloud of gray moths appears in the air,
quick as a light flicked on.
They hover around me like smoke.

Small gray moths.
Fountaining at my shoulders.
Dusting the words I could have said off my lips.

Light gray. Pale as rain. Pale as pills and plastic.

Mamma lets go of her eyelashes, turns her head.
Her frown softens a little. Eyes widen.

I recognize the moths. Not from a textbook or anything. From inside.

When I see them, I know they are made of me.
They have carried something out of me.

A hopelessness as heavy as wet earth.

Everything turns to a slow-thick churn,
bones and stomach and skin.
I stare at the moths. Trying to breathe.

Mamma puts her arms around me.
Squeezes me hard against her ribs.

"I knew your magic would be beautiful," she whispers,
not noticing that I am a hole, opening wider and wider.

Pushes her face against mine. "Soft and gentle and so beautiful.
Look at them, Nell. Just look at them."

I am mortar that won't ever harden.
I am a dark and hungry grave.

But I lean in. Lean towards her. Let her kiss my hair.

The moths thrill and flutter, a thousand little shadows.

Mamma lets go of me. I lose her in all the gray.

Wing-flutter, light-thrill, and the moths start to fall to the ground,
drift down slow to land on the path. Land in the water, carried away.

As they die, the hopeless feeling

pulls its hands
out of me
again.

Until I feel nothing.

My feelings are not only feelings. They are insects.

Mora's blood is not only blood. It is music.

It's supposed to be an addition.

But it feels like something has been taken away.

The day after the gray moths come,
I get a present from my aunt, Sabine, who lives in Germany.

She sends me a box. It arrives in a yellow van.
Mamma, twenty-two, signs for it.

"Are you Nell Strand?" asks the driver.
"I'm Odette. I'm her mother."

I can see the driver looking from Mamma to me,
trying to do the maths in his head.
But he lets her sign and he hands her the box.

I tear it open. For some reason, I am afraid of what's inside.
Mamma watches me. Maybe she is afraid, too.

It's a notebook, lying on a bed of crêpe paper.
The cover is pastel green. The pages remind me of nougat.
There's something rolling in the box, too. A heavy pen.

Mamma looks over my shoulder. "What is it? A journal?"
I close the notebook before she can read the words Sabine wrote in the front:
FOR YOUR SONGS.
In capitals. Like an announcement.
"It's just a notebook," I say.

I've been writing songs for years now.
Songs I play in my room.
Mamma has never asked me about them,
and neither has Dad.
Somehow, only Sabine has noticed.

Sabine, who lives in Germany.

"That's it? Just a notebook? Maybe we need to send Bina some money."

Mamma and Sabine have never been close.

I go to my room, pack the notebook back into the box.
Then I pull it out again and open the front cover.
FOR YOUR SONGS. The ink pressed hard into the paper.
Fast, and with my eyes closed, I shove the box away.

Then I get out
my sheet music
and I sit
at the piano.

I don't play one of my own songs, though.

I need to practice.

Scales, sight-reading,
the piece I was supposed to learn
over the holidays.

My first music lesson of the year
is tomorrow,
and I've been trying
not to think about it,
trying not to think of the small room,
the smooth piano keys.

It doesn't matter how much I practice.
I always feel like I'm losing a battle
that hasn't yet begun.

After the magic comes,
it's like my music teacher,
Mr. _____,
can see it on my skin.

"Something's different about you."

He looks me up and down.

And I don't say anything back
but what I'm thinking is:

something's different about you, too,
something's different about your eyes.

I've been taking music lessons with Mr. _____ for six years now,
and he's always made me feel like his study is a little too small,

but this is the first time
he's looked at me with eyes
like wag-'n-bietjie thorns,

hooking into all the softest places I didn't know I had.

After thirty minutes of piano, there is singing.

I sing   with my back to the door.
I sing   facing the window.
I sing   with three steps of space between my body and Mr. _____'s body.

His face in profile. Reading the music like runes.
His hands, moving over the keys,
his hands on the world and everything in it.

When I leave and he says,
"See you next week,"
my palms are numb and damp,
my cheeks flushed.

The magic happens again on a good day.

On a day when Mamma is twenty-seven.
On a day when Mamma is smiling.

On her smiling days, she uses the word *when*.

When Mora gets better.
When Mora comes home.

We're sitting in her room with mugs of tea
next to the long window
framing the garden like a painting.

Then Mamma looks at me and says:

"I never wanted to have children. I probably shouldn't have had them."

Them. As if *them* isn't *me*.

She stares at the pool that no one swims in anymore.

I act like she isn't talking about me and my sister.
Like she's a friend of my parents,
or a distant relative I don't really know.
Like I'm just a stranger she's confessing to.

"Why did you have them, then?"

"I couldn't do that to your dad. He wanted a family.
And Ouma said—she said I'd be letting him down."

That's when I notice that there is a stick insect on my throat,
slashed across a knot I've been swallowing.

My fingers brush the twig of it.

And there are more of them then.
Crawling slowly along the windowsill.
Crawling up my arms. Sentient pencils.

Sticking my throat with a lead sadness.

They are blue like midnight in summer.
Blue like the freezing sea on cloudless mornings.
Blue like gas-stove flames.

As they walk over my skin, I am immovable as a cave.

Mamma starts to cry, watching the snipped threads of walking blue.
Something passes over her. A shadow crosses the lawn.

"Don't be sad for me, darling," she says.

The stick insects thicken and writhe.
They cover the glassy eye of the window.

"Just look how beautiful you are. Look at your magic.
It suits you so perfectly."

Her mouth at a slant. "Just like your sister's suits her."
She walks out of the room.

Leaves me with the insects.

I close my eyes to feel their feet on my eyelids.

Picture them carried away.

I picture the wind taking them, drifting them over the garden wall.

Picture them, one stretch of subtle blue,
floating over Cape Town like a wind-snatched scarf,
hovering over tarred suburban streets,
over vineyards, patches of scraggly forest,
over dry, scrubby mountains that sit like kindling
waiting to go up in flames.

Picture them finding the sea,
finding black kelp, thick as beams and meaty,
heaped on the sand and rotting.

Picture the stick insects drifting away
and the sadness inside me drifts away, too.
Blue bleached to translucence.

When I open my eyes, they are all dead,
lying on the floor, on the windowsill, in delicate heaps.

In a few weeks,
I will be in Grade 10.

Grade 10
is a foreign country.

When I go there,
I will not know the language.

And I will have to go

alone.

By the middle of Grade 9, I had a friend group.

Not the kind of friends I'd invite to my house.
Just girls to sit with at break. So I didn't have to
hover at the edge of anyone's vision.

We chose a tree in June
and we sat under it
even though it rained every day,
all day, winter clinging to us,
our jerseys damp,
dresses sticking to the backs of our thighs,
downy hair beneath our ponytails curling.

I sat with those girls.
But I could never let them come close.

Some days, they'd try to talk to me
and I'd act like I hadn't heard them.

Whatever was between us
stretched like a strip of elastic.

By the end of the year,
when Mora was admitted to the clinic,
it snapped.

I haven't told Mamma because
I think she will probably say something like:

"That's how all of us Strands are.
We're all misunderstood.
No matter.
You'll survive."

Or she will start to cry and say:
"That's exactly how school was for me."

In my room, I pull the pastel-green notebook
out from under my bed.

It's still lying in its shoebox of paper.

I flip through the pages. Start to sing. Find a melody easily.

Go to the piano and play chords faintly,
my fingers barely pressing the keys down.
Words cling to the melody like sugar to fingertips.
And I want to write the words down.
I want to write in the notebook Sabine gave me.
With the heavy pen she left nestled in the box.
Like she was saying, "The songs you write.
They mean something. They have weight."

But the blue stick insects appear again,
crawling around my throat, tightening it.

In nests like bundles of pine needles,
they are slow over the piano's keys, then still,
the sadness suspended in front of me,
sitting on ivory, thin as filaments.

And then the sadness cracks open inside me.
My throat is closed, and I can't sing anymore.
The stick insects fill my small white room, weightless, crowding the window.

They fill the room
until everything I see
is a different shade of blue.

They are on my lips. Moving against my eyelids.

Just when I think the room
can't hold any more of them,
they begin to die,

make a carpet
on the wooden floor.

When I am sure they are not alive.
When the sadness is gone, replaced by an unmoving, unliving numbness,
I fetch a broom and sweep them into a pile.

I carry them outside in handfuls, scattering them in the flower beds.

I pack the notebook and the pen away. Slide the box out of sight.

I'm supposed to be practicing
but I stuff my sheet music in a drawer
and slam the lid of the piano.

I call Sabine instead.

Her face fills the screen,
her hair shaved all the way down to pale fuzz.

"Did you get my present?"
"I did. Thanks."
"Written anything yet?"
Long pause. "I've been busy."
She smiles. Knows I'm lying. "How're things going?" she says.

Sabine moved to Germany when she was nineteen

because she needed
some distance
from the family.

That's the story I grew up with, anyway.

I didn't realize why she needed the distance until I was older.

Now I know it's because her hair
has a habit of whispering secrets.
And knowing your family's secrets—all of them,
whether you want to or not—
makes living with them impossible.

My secrets are safe, though,
when I talk to her on the phone.
The screen does something to the magic.
Her hair can't read me from here.

Sometimes I wish she was in the room with me.
And sometimes I am relieved she isn't.

"Did your magic come yet?"

I tell her about the stick insects.
The ladybugs. The moths.

"That's so interesting," she says. I can tell she really means it.

Silence squeezes between us, though.

"Are you worried about when it happens again?" she asks.
"I mean, it probably will? Definitely will. I don't have any control over that."
"I know. But that's not what I asked." She tilts her head.
"It's okay, Sabine. You don't have to counsel me."
"I'm just curious. I know it can be hard. To adjust."

It feels good to have someone be curious. Sabine is the only one who ever is.
But it also feels dangerous. I get the urge to hang up.

"I've got to go practice," I say.
"Okay. Chat to you soon, ja?"

She smiles widely
right up until
I push the button.

"Just come," says Mamma.
"You're coming. We're going to try again."

She's older today: thirty-four.

And thirty-four gives her sentences edges.

Sit in the car. Silent. Forehead pressed against the window.

The world going by, green and shadow,
dry heat, graying tarmac,
till we pull into the parking area at the clinic.

The oak trees shading the cars
are probably as old as Cape Town.

They dig their roots
under the bricks
and lift them,
loosen them like teeth.

Inside, Mamma talks to the woman
behind the reception desk.

She says our name: "Strand."
"Stranded?" says the woman.
"No. Strand. As in the Afrikaans word for beach?"

I don't blame the woman for being confused.

Mamma doesn't say our name
like it's an Afrikaans word.
She says it in the English way,
so that it rhymes with *stand* or *land*.

Mamma says everything the English way.
Most people don't even know she's Afrikaans.

When she was seventeen,
she decided
that she didn't want to speak it anymore.

She married an English man and raised two English children,
like she wanted to cut herself off from something—
some shameful thing she could only say in her mother's tongue.

In my mind,
beaches and loneliness,
being left behind,
they've always gone together.

Mamma didn't think about how,
when she cut herself off from something,
she left us without it, too.

And now the history
that only language carries
is a window
of scratched glass.

Mora's eyes are glazed.

I'm holding my breath. Waiting for her to scream.
But she doesn't scream.
It's worse, what she does. Looks through me,
past me, over my shoulder, at the cream wall.

"Mora," says Mamma. She tries to sound strict, but it comes out like a plea.
"Say hello to your sister."

"Hey, traitor."

She's still not looking at me. She's looking beyond, behind,
through the wall and over the hilly, tree-lined roads, over all the houses.

Her eyes are on the blue summer sea, ice cold and knife-bright.
I can see the water in her eyes. I can see it churning.

My sister's blood is an orchestra.
Inside her, music lives.

Picture the sea in the evening. Rushing at you like a predator.
Imagine how deep it is. Beyond where you can see. Fins and teeth.
Picture the water. Pooling around sun-touched rocks.

When you grow up near the sea, they tell you:
never turn your back to the waves. The waves here are not gentle.
They do not lap like kittens. They roar, crash; they are shatter-white.
Violent enough to splinter your shin bones.
There are great white sharks in the water. No nets. No separations.
At any moment, you could be swallowed, or split in half.

They tell you: do not swim in the evening.
They tell you not to go in too deep.
The sea is beautiful. The sea will probably kill you.

That is what my sister is like. That's what her music is like.

"That wasn't so bad," says Mamma,

driving home from the clinic,
driving her car fast,
younger every second.

Her face changes and changes
like flipped magazine pages.
I can't fix it still with my eyes.

Press my forehead against the cool window.
Tree trunks. Quivering branches. Green-shadowed tar.
The sun slowly swallowed up by the blue mountain.

Faces and faces and faces.

For two whole days, Mamma is fifteen.
She drives to the shops dressed in her pajamas,
her hair tangled in a bun.
It's a miracle she doesn't get pulled over.

She buys a huge carrot cake and drops it on the kitchen counter.
As if she's trying to make up for what happened on my birthday,
how she walked out the house with icing still on her fingers.

"We're going to eat cake for the weekend," she says.

Nod once. Slowly.

This would never happen if Dad were home.
But he's gone away. Work trip.

Mamma makes presentation hands at the cake.
Then she looks at me. Shrugs. Like she's lost interest in all of it:
the cake and me and everything.

"If you're hungry," she calls as she walks away.

She stays in bed most of Saturday,
except when she comes downstairs
to drink wine out of a teacup
and watch British reality TV shows.

I stare at my phone for hours,
not even knowing what I'm checking it for.

We eat half the cake by the time Dad gets back.

When he drops his suitcase on the floor, I want to hug him,

but he's not the hugging type.

"What's for dinner?" he says, glancing at the cake.

He orders takeout from the Italian place down the road.

On Monday morning,

when I wake up,

Mamma is sweeping

the kitchen floor.

In her thirties again.

I'm so relieved I can't speak.

"So each of the insects," says Sabine. "They're a different feeling?"

I nod. Then I feel like I'm lying.

"I don't feel anything, though."

"What do you mean?"

When I'm quiet, Sabine doesn't rush to speak.
She keeps her eyes on me. To tell me she wants to hear it.
Wants to hear what I have to say.

"I mean. A lot of the time.
I guess I must have feelings.
I must be feeling something.
But I don't notice.
I don't feel like I'm feeling anything.
And then, when they come—
when the insects come—
I watch them for a bit.
And I can see what I'm feeling.
When before—I didn't know.
It's like I have inside-blindness."

This makes Sabine laugh
and she starts to say something
but then her face pixelates
on the screen, scatters
before showing whole again.

When she comes back, she says,
"That actually sounds kind of helpful."
Her voice lags and crackles.

"It's horrible," I say.
"Because as soon as I see the feeling—
as soon as I see the insects. And I know what the feeling is.
I can actually—feel it."
I squirm, sitting on the end of my bed.
"Sometimes it hurts."

That word—*hurts*—gets something out of me.
Right in front of Sabine.
A blue stick insect pops into view,
clinging to my chest,
and a stinging line crosses my heart
like a thin crack in porcelain.

Sabine squints. "Nell," she says. "I'm sorry.
That was flippant of me."

The stick insect falls in my lap, dead.
The sadness dies with it.

"But do you think," Sabine says,
"that maybe this magic
could be good for you?"

She says it gently. Like she knows it's a sharp sort of truth.

"I don't know. Maybe.
But it also makes things harder."

"Ja. I get that."

"But for now, it's okay.
And anyway—I can't do anything about it."

"Sure," she says. "But what you're feeling about it. That still matters."

"I guess." I look away from the screen. Rub my eyes. "It's fine. I'm fine."

"Okay."

"You don't believe me? Sabine. I'm always fine."

"You are," she says. "But you don't have to be. You know that, right?"

And I want to laugh. But I hold it in.

I dream about Mr. _____.

Dream I am closed in a cupboard with him,
and no matter which way I turn,
my arm is always touching his arm,
my leg is always pressed against his leg.
There's a sound coming from inside the cupboard.
A screech. Swarming. A growing growl.

The more I try to move away,
the smaller the cupboard gets.
Wood pressed against my cheek.
Splinters in my elbows from trying to get free.

Mr. _____ turns to me and smiles.
In the dim glow, his teeth look like piano keys.

"I've never noticed before."
"Noticed what?"
"How pretty you are."

My eyes open in the dark.
The dream has left me like a tide pulling out.

I hear hard shells flicking themselves against floorboards.
Lunge for my bedside lamp.

On the floor
there is a crawling heap
of glossy beetles,
plump and long-legged.

Sit up. Pull my knees in. Press the back of my skull to the headboard.
I close my eyes. "Please. Please."
I don't want to look at the beetles. I don't want to recognize them.
Don't want to feel whatever it is they want me to feel.

When I open my eyes, though, the beetles are still there,
their sticky legs trailing the smooth floor. Still writhing. Still alive.

They are crawling over the cashmere blanket
folded neatly at the foot of my bed.

I grab it and shake it, toss it on the floor.
I don't want them anywhere near me.

Even if
they were
once
a part of me.

Even if
they are
still
a part of me.

Then a glimpse of the dream comes back.

The cupboard.
Teeth like old ivory.

I don't want to look at the beetles.
But I recognize them anyway. Even if I shut my eyes.

The heat of shame.

The beetles die on the floor,
some of them still stuck together.

The feeling, the clench of it, dies with them.

When they have stopped moving,
I walk to the kitchen in the dark,
fetch the broom and the skeppie.

I sweep them up, dump them into the bin.

With the rotten pawpaw.
The ceramic shards of a bowl
Mamma broke at lunch.
With the dust and the hair and the tea bags.

So I guess
Sabine and I
are kind of similar.

Her hair
tells her things
she doesn't want to know.

My insects
show me things
I don't want to feel.

Of course I have to go to a music lesson the day after the beetles come.

While Mamma is driving me there,
I keep seeing flashes of Mr. ____ and me in a cupboard,
my mouth jammed against his shoulder.

The car pulls to a stop.

Mamma is listening to her favorite rock band.
She's putting on pale lipstick in the rearview mirror.
She's twenty-five today. Bobbing her head.

It takes me four seconds to hear her. "Nell. Are you getting out?"

I nod and open the door, spill onto the pavement like sticky juice.

Mamma drives off, leaves me standing on the curb.

I walk up the shaded path to the front door,
squashing rotting flowers under my sandals.

When I stand in the doorway,
Mr. _____ knows I'm there without having to turn around.
He's scribbling. Hunched over his desk.
Head bowed. Like he's writing something important.
Writing something down that he never wants to forget.

He doesn't turn.

"Nell."

Says my name like he has discovered it.

"Come in. Come here."

He doesn't stop waving me over until I am right at his side,
squeezed between the elbow of the piano and the corner of the desk.

He puts his arm around me. His waving hand rests on my hip.
His fingers stroke the band of skin between my jeans and T-shirt.

I look down. At his desk.

I want to see what he was doing.
What he was writing.
The thing that was so important.

So important it couldn't wait, he couldn't get out of his chair,
he had to wave me over, and I had to walk to him,
approach him from behind, and he had to put his arm around me,
cup the ridge of my hip bone in his hand.

He is writing nothing.

He is erasing an appointment off his desk calendar.

Writing it again. Neater this time.

He pats my side twice and releases his hand.

Hand across my back. His fingers twitch.

"Time to warm up," he says.

And I am left with the feeling of his skin on my skin.

Like I am new, wet clay. Like every touch leaves a mark.

It's evening when the lesson is over.

I sit on the curb,
waiting for Mamma.

The sun sinks, turning the windows to mirrors.

I sit there for half an hour before I message her.

Where are you?

I've been waiting for ages

Hello?

In the end, I phone Dad, and he comes straight away.

"What happened?" I ask.

Dad puts the car into gear.

"Mamma's staying with Ouma for a little while."

"Why?"

He looks ahead as he pulls off.

"She's feeling overwhelmed right now."

The full stop at the end of the sentence is a nail hammered into a wall.

So I don't ask
any more questions.

My dad is a good driver.
One of those people who enjoys driving.
As if it's a sport or a hobby,
not just a way of getting around.
My dad could steer a ship if he wanted to.

He is his own map.
Own compass.

His car is clean. No coins or chewing gum wrappers.
No disposable coffee cups. Always smells new.

It makes me think of school.
How it's starting soon.
School always gives me
a cold, gray feeling,
like I've swallowed river water.

Occasionally,
Dad would take us to school
when we were little.
Grade 1 and Grade 2.

He would drop us off so early
that the grounds would still be empty and dark,
Egyptian geese asleep on the dew-pale field,
their long necks tucked around their bodies.

As soon as we got there, Mora would leave me,
walking through stretching shadows
towards her classroom.

But the thing I remember
most about those mornings
was how Dad flinched
when we climbed in the car,
worried the buckles of our school shoes
would scratch the leather seats.

Now I sit with my palms clasped,
making myself small. Stare ahead.

The dark and the quiet sit inside me
like a cat in a window.

Dad turns on the radio. He's not wondering what I am thinking.
He doesn't know that I am a girl filled with the darkening world.
He is watching his headlights. Carrying us both to safety.

The first thing I do when I get home is call Mamma.

I can hear how young she is,
how she's gotten younger
since I saw her in the afternoon.

"Can I come see you?" I say.

There is a sound like swallowed wool.

"No. I don't think that's a good idea, darling.
I'll be home in a few days. You'll be fine."

I hang up and sit down.
"I'll be fine," I say to the wall. "I'll be fine."

"Did something happen? With Mamma?"

Dad shakes his head.

Meaning: Have you looked around lately?
Meaning: Where have you been these past few months?
Meaning: Don't ask me to tell you. Don't ask me to say it out loud.

Dad drops me off at Ouma's house on Saturday.

Because I ask him to.
Because maybe he likes the idea of going against what Mamma said.
Because maybe he doesn't want to argue.
Because he doesn't have time for that.
Because he's far too busy to get in the middle of things.
Because he's far too busy for anything that is happening to me.

My ouma's house hides
behind an enormous avocado tree.

57 Paradise Crescent.
She calls it an Edwardian gem.

Her favorite possession in the world is a letter
that her father received from Queen Elizabeth II.
She keeps it folded in a wooden box,
its central crease wearing away,
splitting one half from the other.
She pulls it out every so often. To show me.
To say, "We don't all hate the English. See?"

I ring the bell, listening to Dad's car
traveling further and further down the road.

Ouma opens the door,
holding Hildegarde.

"Hey, Hildegarde," I say.

"Liefie," says Ouma. She pulls me in with her free arm
and kisses me on the head.

A single blue stick insect brushes my throat,
thin as a strand of spider's silk.
I let it walk onto the back of my hand.
An ashy sadness burns in my chest.

Ouma pulls away a little, watches the insect.
"You got your magic," she says tenderly.

"Where's Mamma?" I say.
I don't want to talk about my magic.

I flick the stick insect off my hand and it falls to the ground,
dying on the black-and-white marble.
The ash in my chest turns to solid, smooth stone.

Ouma pauses. I can see she's going somewhere in her mind.
"My bedroom," she says.

"Can I go up?"

"Let me make you a cup of tea first." Patting my wrist,
wrapping her fingers around it, leading me to the kitchen.

I'm relieved there are no more insects.
But Hildegarde is sniffing the air, struggling to get closer to me.
Like she knows I've changed.

Ouma makes tea.

Three Five Roses tea bags in the pot.
The click of the electric kettle.

After the pot has brewed,
she fills three cups of rusty tea with milk,
turning them three shades of reddish pink:
almond, sand, cinnamon.

We sit outside, in the courtyard.
A rectangle of amber stone,
lush with watered ferns.

Ouma sips her tea and strokes Hildegarde.
"Are you all ready for school to start soon?"

"Not really," I tell her.

She closes her eyes.

"She'll come down soon," she says, patting my hand again.
"She heard your daddy's car."

Ouma's magic:

when she's inside a building,
it's as if the building shrinks down
to the size of a dollhouse,
gets crammed behind her ribs.

Every room is inside her. Every sound in every room.
Every texture. Every windowed slant of light.

When she's inside your house,
it's like she has swallowed it,
and everything that lives inside it
lives inside her, too,
moving in her mind in real time.

The temperature of each room is a shimmer of heat,
a rush of cold in her body.

The cat, creeping across the kitchen floor:
she can feel its footsteps.

You can never do anything in secret
while Ouma is in the house.

She knows if you write your name on the wall.
If you scratch a mark in a writing desk.

She can feel the rattle of old hangers.
Drawers opened, coins pocketed when no one is looking.

When you open a window. She can't help but draw in a breath.

Of course I think about Ouma
when I think
about everything I must have inside me.
The wings. The swarming.
Humming. Stick-sting-glimmer. Rising clouds
I don't have names for yet.

I think of Ouma when I don't know what I will do with myself.
With all the life in me. All the most difficult magic.

Mamma finally comes downstairs
wearing a silk robe
she pulled from Ouma's wardrobe,
fifteen and freshly teary,
streaks of mascara on her cheeks.

I've finished my tea
and Hildegarde has disappeared
down a path of moss-softened stones.

Mamma's face is as white as the arum lilies
in her wedding photographs.

"Nell," she says, not surprised and not angry.
She starts to cry, doesn't hug me, ignores the cup of tea
Ouma made for her, which is now cold.

She sits on the other end of the table.
Tears are running down her cheeks
like cheap watercolors.

Ouma says something in Afrikaans that I don't catch.
Hildegarde is barking. No one tells her to be quiet.

I get up.

I don't know where I'm going
but I have to get out of the house.

Mamma calls out after me.

Ouma says, "Let her go."

Let me go.

My shoulders say it,
my back, the nape of my neck.

I walk through
the cool of the house.
Walk out the front door and stand, restless,
beneath the avocado tree,
looking up through its generous leaves.

Then I start up the hill, walking past the houses
that wind towards Newlands Forest. I walk and I walk, huffing.

I walk through the little gate
leading into the forest reserve.

The steep road is fanned
with oak trees, but the forest is all
thick-wooded pine.

Trees tall enough
to be wise.

I want to ask them something.
I want to tell them. Something.

"Please—"

Three steps into the forest.
Into the trees, and they come. They come,
exploding. Wasps. A swarm of them.
Moving around like a current.
When I look up, breathing like a trapped animal,
they have swallowed the trees around me.
They have swallowed the sky.
I don't know what to do but kneel.
This. All of this. Belongs to me.
These dark wings, this sound, this danger.
The anger breaks open inside me.
Something thaws. There is fire underneath.
Hot as white sand in summer. Muscular as storms.
It rips through me. It takes all my strength to stay there,
hunched under the swell. To stay, to watch them,
spreading through the trees. The anger, my anger—
old anger, and new—rages and ranges through me.
Eventually, the wasps stop droning,
stop buzzing, and they die.
They fall to the ground,
heavy as pebbles.
And the feeling fades.
Simmering sea cools.
I wait in the silence of the forest
for the courage to move again.

Eyes burning, I get up.
I feel nothing now. Nothing again.

Walk back to Ouma's house. Down the cobbled hill.

I never want that to happen again.
I never want that to happen. Again.

I can't even say the word *wasp*. Word like injury.
Walk, and breathe, and listen
to the sound of my feet, and they say, they are saying,
"Never-never. Never."

I never want to feel that again.

I pass the avocado tree. Get to the doorstep.
Slip through the door like a dog who's run away and come back.

There are streaks of dirt on the backs of my hands.
Like I've fought with something and won.

That is the thing
I choose to remember.

PART TWO

NINE DAYS AFTER THE WASPS

I count my life in apples.

One apple for breakfast.
One apple for lunch.

Hunger dampens everything, like a pedal on a piano.
Like thick curtains drawn over sunlit windows.
Earth heaped over green leaves.

Hunger
keeps
the insects
inside.

The clinic calls to say
we're set to start family therapy with Mora.
They think it'll be helpful.
They recommend the entire family attend.

Dad says, "Really? All of us?"

He hasn't set foot inside Cressida Clinic
and I don't think he wants to change that.

Mamma and Dad talk about it at dinner,
an argument that never gets loud
then stops abruptly, like someone muting the TV.

I scrape my dinner into the bin and go to bed.
Lie with my head under the duvet. Hoping. For dreamless sleep.
Hoping. I won't wake up. To a room full of wings.

So far. The apples are working.

I haven't seen another wasp since that day in the forest.
No moths, no stick insects. Not a single ladybug.
Even the beetles have stayed away.

When I walk, I feel like I'm hovering a little bit above the ground.
Filled with air. Balloon-girl.

I am in the world.
But the world.
Doesn't get to come near me.

Some days
I even forget
that I have magic.

What the apples give me:

a sheet over everything,
white and clean,
muffling the mouth of the magic.

Doesn't mean it'll never come back.
Doesn't mean the wings won't come.

They'll always—

Eventually, they'll come.

Things Mamma says to me when she's older:

"Have you eaten today? I made toasties."

"It's time to tidy up."

"Sometimes we don't choose what happens to us.
We just have to try to live with it."

"Everything passes eventually, Nell."

"One day you'll look back and realize how beautiful you are now.
Try to remember that."

"The whole world is just light, Nell. Light, playing with our eyes."

When Mamma is thirty-three. Thirty-eight. Forty-one and forty-two.
She quotes Haruki Murakami and Marc Chagall.
She does pliés in the kitchen, using the counter as a barre.
She reads with her feet tucked under her on the sofa.
She laughs. She buys big white boxes of blueberry muffins.

Sometimes, she rests a hand on my head for a few seconds,

just to show
that she's noticing.

Things Mamma says to me
when she's younger/young/too young to be my mother:

"Some people are mirrors, Nell.
Always looking to others to tell them how they should act.
They don't have their own form.
They just reflect what's going on around them.
That's how you are."

"One day, you're going to wake up in the morning
and find me gone. Then what will you do?"

"It was always easier to love you
than it was to love your sister."

"I was chubby, too, you know.
I grew out of it, though. Thank God."

"There are only so many times
you can forgive someone."

"Leave me alone."
"Leave me alone."
"Leave me alone."

"Nell. I'm fine. Just leave me alone."

"You know, if you wanted to lose some weight—
a slice of lemon in boiling water. It really helps."

"That's a nice top. No doubt some boy is going to want to take it off you."

(Later, I remembered I'd worn the top to a music lesson.
Beetles crawled over my shoulders and down my back like a dripping cape.
Smacked by so much shame I had to sit down.)

"Go away," Mamma says.

"I don't want to talk about it."

"I said I don't want to talk about it."

"Please. Go away."

"I just can't deal with you right now, Nell."

These days.
Mamma is fifteen.
Sixteen.
Seventeen.
A lot.

At family therapy
the air conditioner is louder than us all,
blustering like an old man,
a man even older than the psychiatrist.
Dr. Doesn't See Me.

Dad doesn't want to be here,
keeps pulling his phone out of his pocket.

Mamma wants to be here.
She's forty-two today.

I love her face when she's forty-two.
When faint blue veins embroider her eyes.

Even her voice is different,
like she's testing what she says before it comes out.
Like she's not actually so sure about everything.
I love her intensely, brightly, in the dull psychiatrist's office.

Even if
she doesn't
look at me
once.

Mora is slumped in her chair,
staring at the ceiling, pretending she's alone.

Mora's music, wrapped up silent within her:

I imagine it
pressing like hands
against the small windows
from outside.

The psychiatrist asks Mamma questions,
asks Dad questions. Talks to Mora.

But he doesn't talk to me.

It wasn't always like this.

When we were little, really little,
Mora and I were close,
stuck together like letters of the alphabet.
First comes *M*, then comes *N*.
People used to call us L-M-N-O.
Because Mamma's name is Odette,
and Dad's name is Leon.

And there we were,
two girls,
Mora and Nell,
in the middle.

For whole years, we believed we were mermaids.

We used to swim in the pool until evening,
till the water turned purple like the sky.

Mora stopped swimming after she got her magic.

I swam alone after that.

It was strange without her.
The trees crowded the edge of the pool
and I was afraid of the deep end,
the water always so much colder than I thought it would be.

Before Mora got her magic,
I would dive into that cold,
and from the bottom of the pool I would look up
at the branch-broken surface. Just to show her.

But after she stopped swimming.
There was no one to pretend for anymore.
Mora hated me for telling Mamma,
and when I swam,
sometimes I caught her watching
from her bedroom window,
watching like I was the enemy.

That's when I gave up on the water.

"Ready for school?" Mamma asks.

I'm not ready for the fact
that I haven't spoken to anyone from school
since the end of Grade 9.

For the truth that I actually don't have any friends,
and never really did.

I'm not ready to start Grade 10.
Not ready for the questions about Mora.

And now I have to worry about wasps, too.
Beetles and moths and stick insects.

But Mamma is young today,
painfully young, as young as me.

Her face is smooth and white,
her eyes half-closed,
nightgown stuck to her sweating back,
delicate bones underneath.
Thinner than she's ever been.

I hand her the cup of tea I made her
and shake my head. "I'm ready," I say.

"Can you walk to school? Dad had an early meeting."

I don't tell her I already knew that.

When I woke up,
his empty coffee cup
was sitting in the sink.

I pack my things and put on my uniform.

Checked blue dress,
dark-blue jersey,
brown leather shoes,
short white socks for summer.

My bag is heavy with books.

I feel like I'm carrying everything that's happened
over the holidays.

There's nowhere to put it. I can't give it to anyone—
not to Mora, or Mamma, or Dad, or Ouma. Not to Sabine.

So I take it with me.

At school, a boy corners me at the top of the stairs.

The passage I'm trying to get to is full of kids my age,
blasting music on their phones, shouting,
throwing rugby balls, playing games of cricket.

The boy at the top of the stairs has sticky eyes,
licks at the air like a dog.

Under my heavy bag, under my scratchy jersey,
I can feel a beetle crawling. Squeezing its way along my spine.
The boy laughs. Push past him, walk up the last three steps.

Catch a girl's eye.
But she's laughing, too.

"Don't pretend you're a prude," she says,
aiming the words at the girls arcing around her like a retinue.
"Everyone knows you love the attention."

I don't even know her.
But she thinks she knows Mora.
So she thinks she knows me, too.

I walk to the end of the passage
and sit on the floor,
pulling my bag onto my lap.

Unbutton the front of my dress
and stick my hand through the gap,
reaching around my side
for the beetle. Cup it in my hand
and pull it off my skin, pull my jersey down
over the open button. I watch the beetle.
Shame oozes inside me.

Everyone knows. You love the attention.

I wait until the beetle dies.

Then I put it in my pencil case so I can get rid of it later.

We all file into one of the biology classrooms
to listen to our names being read.
The teacher has frizzy blond hair
and a serious face. Flat eyebrows and a sharp jaw.

When she calls my name
and I raise my hand, she says,
"Are you Mora's sister?"
I nod, feeling the whole class
turn to look at me.

Mrs. Coetzee sighs, her eyes aimed at her clipboard, widening.

"Well," she says. "Let's hope it doesn't run in the family."

I walk along the scraggly hem of the field
to drop the dead beetle in the bin.

Then I go to the tap, run my hands under water.

There are a few Grade 11 boys playing soccer
in their school shoes, ties loose around their necks.

One of them stops running when he sees me.
Lifts his hand and waves. "Hey," he says, out of breath.

I think he's going to say something else,
but he doesn't. Just looks at me for a second,
smiling a little, then goes back to playing.

I watch him, his shirt shaped against him as he runs.
He's beautiful. His hair is curly, like mine.

The way he looked at me. Is the opposite of a sticky beetle.
The way he looked at me. Is like light poured over stone.

After another night of family therapy,
we drive home, moving through darkness
like a submarine moves through water.

Dad, behind the wheel: "I don't know what the point of that was."

Mamma opens her mouth. Waits. "I don't know either."

I sit in the middle of the back seat. Between them. Knees up, eyes forward.

It always used to be me at one window and Mora at the other.
Me humming to myself. Mora pointing out things she saw.

The world rolled by before our eyes but I don't think we saw the same thing.

The dark is too thick to look out the window now.

To watch the world
through Mora's window
or through mine.

So I look ahead, at what Dad can always see:

two straight lines of light
cutting through the murk

to get us home.

The next afternoon,
Mr. _____ is touching my hair.

He hooks two fingers into my ponytail
while I'm playing the piano. Doing a sight-reading exercise.

I am hopeless at sight-reading.

"Try again," he says. Gentle voice. Sits on the stool beside me.

Hot hand. Hot skin of my thigh.

I take my sticky hands off the keys and tug at the hem
of my school dress. Hot hand. Hot fabric. His palm burning through cotton.

I can feel him watching me, eyes hard.
But I don't look. Pretend to read the notes.

He pulls his hand away, moves back to the desk.

Do I want the attention?

Turn around.
Look at me. Smile. Tell me you're not angry.
Tell me you're not angry with me.
I want the attention. I must want it.

A feeling gets free of me:

three desperate, buzzing flies,
throwing their bodies against the window.

Mr. _____ frowns at them.

I'm looking at them, too. Desperation echoes inside me.
I want to throw myself against glass.

But I bite my lip. Turn back to the music.
And the flies stop buzzing. They die on the windowsill.

I ask Mr. _____ if I can go to the bathroom.

Lock the door behind me and stare at my face in the mirror.
My eyes are asking something. But the rest of me is blank.

My insides are nothing but white noise.
Traffic from far away. Wind in the branches of trees.
I take a long time to wash my hands.

When I open the door again,
I expect him to be there. Waiting for me. But he isn't.

I look left, up a carpeted passage, away from his study.
I don't think. I'm not thinking. The static in my heart makes the choice.

I walk up the passage. Away from the piano.

I find myself in Mr. _____'s bedroom.
It has mirrored cupboards with no handles. It has a bed with lilac covers.
Stand there for a second. Looking around.

The mirrored doors don't have a single smudge or mark.

I catch my eyes in one of them.
Another face appears. Beside mine.

I've always known she was there.
I've always known he had a wife.
But she's always been in another room,
down the hall, in the kitchen,
a voice I could only ever hear from a distance.

Up until now,
I didn't know I was looking for her.
That I wanted to see her, to test her,
to know she was real.

I wanted to know
there was someone else
in the house
besides me and him.

She's folding a dishcloth in her hands,
eyes asking some sort of question.

"I'm sorry," I say. Slip past her. Out the door.
Leave her standing there. She doesn't call after me.

"You were in the bathroom for a long time," says Mr. _____.
Frowning like he's disappointed. "We only have five minutes left."

I close the door behind me.
I sing with my back against it.

"Come closer," he says. Laughing.
"You're not scared of me. Are you?"

My sister walks around
with an orchestra inside her.

An orchestra
she's not allowed
to let out.

The only way she knows
how to hear the music

is to hurt herself.

My sister walks around
with an orchestra inside her.

Violins sawing.
Thin voices of clarinets.

When she cuts herself,
she can hear this part of her
singing in terrifying harmony.

But then the cuts heal and she goes back
to keeping it all inside.

It must hurt
to keep a universe
against your ribs.

That kind of aching.

It can make you do things.

You never thought.

You never thought you'd do.

"I heard they locked your sister up."

"I heard she's in an asylum."

"She's a drug addict, right?"

"Your sister is a slut."

"She had a threesome."

"Your sister is fucked."

"She's been with everyone."

"She bunked so much school, they won't let her come back."

"Your sister punched a teacher."

"I don't think she went to class once."

"You're Mora's sister? I didn't know she had a sister."

"You're Mora's sister? You're hot."

"Mora used to be hot. Until. You know."

"She used to be the coolest girl in school."

"She was a riot."

"Did you hear she started a fire in Mr. Joubert's classroom?"

"Of course. You must have heard that. You were here, too."

"You're only a year apart?"

"Oh, I remember you. I forgot she had a sister who goes here."

"You're such a nerd."

"Mora must hate you."

"I didn't realize how similar you looked until now."

"Where's Mora now?"

"What's Mora up to?"

"Where's Mora?"

"It was always going to end badly. She's just that kind of girl."

My school is all gray inside.

In some places
the windows are so small,
the spaces so lightless and squeezed,
it feels like we are underground.

In these shadow spaces,
I pass the boy.

The boy in Grade 11.
The boy who waved.
The boy who said, "Hey."

One time, because he's new and always getting lost,
he stops me and says, "Do you know how to get to Lab B?"

He's got a highlighted timetable stuck to the back of his file.

"No," I say, and walk away, fast.

Once, when I'm looking for the boy—
trying to look like I'm not looking—
I bump into Saskia, Mora's ex–best friend.

For a second, we're still, looking at each other,
and I want to say that I don't blame her—

for not visiting,
for turning away.

I want to tell her I would take that option, too, if I could.

I want to tell her that her hair looks nice.

But she looks at me like I am a piece of art she saw in a museum once,
a pleasant sight that didn't make much of an impression.

She walks away, and my chance to speak is gone.

After a long, blurry day, my head full of Mora,
Ouma fetches me from school.

I'm waiting for ages,
looking out for Mamma's car,
when I notice Ouma sitting in her shining old Mercedes.
Dappled shade over her face like a veil.

"Something happened," she says when I open the heavy car door.
"Your mamma asked me to fetch you."

I slide onto the cool seat.

"Are you hungry?" she says.

"No." This is a lie and not a lie.

I definitely need to eat. I do not feel hungry.

We sit under the swaying shade of the trees,
both of us looking ahead
through the car's clean windshield,
both of us aware of my lie that isn't precisely a lie,
until Ouma turns the key in the ignition.

My ouma's skin is so flawless, so smooth and pale,
that often people assume she's my mother.

But she doesn't have Mamma's magic. That belongs to Odette Strand alone.

That's part of it: the magic doesn't have a path.

We can't make sense of it. With every girl, it's new.

No tradition. No circling back.

Fresh, blank page. Every time. The loneliness of it.

And only this: figure it out. Figure out how to survive as you.

Figure it out. Before it ruins you.

The clinic is as quiet
and clean as it always is.

Like the walls take all the screaming
the rooms have heard
and suffocate it
behind beige paint.

Ouma talks to the receptionist.

We wait,
and wait.

Ouma opens a magazine.
Closes it. Sighs.

I can see she's struggling with this place.
All the walls and windows and doors.
All the rooms. All the walls and windows
and doors and rooms. All inside her.

Ouma doesn't leave the house often.

It's hard to move through the world
when the world goes right through you.

When you feel every footstep,
every opened window, every slammed door,
every shout and breath and dirty mop,
shivering through you,
a hundred movies playing at once.

That's why she can't go to a mall.
That's why she never went to university.

Ouma's favorite place is home.
Her favorite way to move is to read.

She's always said it's the only way to fly. But I think what she means is
it's the only way she's ever flown.

"I'll just wait until your mamma comes," she says to me.

Mamma appears at the back of the room
like she's been standing there for ages.
Light glistens around her like dew. She's barely older than me.

She waves us over, takes Ouma's hand and squeezes it.

"She nearly died," she says.

Mora's arms are all bandaged up. I try not to look at her for long.

Her eyes slide
past me, to Mamma,
to the window.

Beyond it. The oak trees. Shuffling their young green leaves.

Everything has started over.
But the three of us are stuck here, motionless.

Rooms like this. They don't know about the seasons.

"It wasn't just her arms," Mamma says in the car. "It was her stomach, too."

"Stitches," she says. "They had to stitch her up."

"They don't know how she got the razor blade."

"Maybe she stole it," she says. "Maybe someone gave it to her."

"Obviously no one's going to tell me if they did."

I stare ahead at the unfolding road.

And the car   does not fill   with any kind of wing.

My sister nearly died.
And this is ordinary.

She almost died
and this is ordinary life.

At home, we eat without speaking.

Mamma doesn't even sit down.

She leans against the kitchen counter, eyes unfocused on the wall.

I can't make myself swallow.

The world.
The whole world.
The width of Mora's door.

The next day,

Mamma is in the study with the door half-closed,
pacing along the border of the Persian carpet,
her phone tucked against her ear.

I can tell she's in her early twenties.

I can tell she's talking to Sabine.

"You're not here. You don't get to tell me what's going on in my family—"
"No, that's not what I said."
"You don't. You don't know what it's like."
"She's my child."

She is Mora. *She* is always Mora. Never me.

The talking stops
and Mamma comes out,
stands in front of me
with her arms crossed.
"You know she only calls you
to get the family gossip.
So she can use it against me."

I want to say
that when Sabine calls
she asks about me
and I tell her the truth,
which isn't the same as gossiping.

I want to say that Sabine is just worried—
worried about Mora, like we all are.

With one difference: Sabine is also worried about me.

Before I can open my mouth, though,
Mamma has walked away,
clutching her phone like it's a brick
she's preparing to throw.

And I know that even if I followed her.
I wouldn't be able to find her.

It's Mr. _____'s hand on my neck that makes it happen again.
Even though I've only eaten a single apple today.

First, a sticky black beetle
sits like a jewel against my throat.

And then

a wasp
gets free
of me.

"Jesus," says Mr. _____, ducking.

I peel the beetle from my skin,
throw it on the ground while he's not looking.
I wipe the palm of my hand on my skirt.
My heart is glue and honey.

Then the wasp buzzes.

I stare at it; I can't help but stare at it.
I am a tunnel full of heat.
I have swallowed a line of small fires.

I look at Mr. _____,
and, for a second,
I want to leave the room,
slam the door.
I want to scream.

But before I do any of that
the wasp dies
in midair,
falls onto the carpet,
unmoving.

The fires
are snuffed out,
sugar and chemicals
scorched away.

And I go back to feeling like an empty container.

But the part of me
that was fire,
that was burning,
that was unafraid,
is still there,
lying on the carpet,
small and dark.

Real.

I turn back to the piano.

Mamma is late to pick me up,
and I can't help worrying
that she's gone to stay at Ouma's again.

I sit on Mr. _____'s lawn.

On the curb first,
then on the path that cuts the lawn
in two.

I make agreements with myself.

If she comes at 5:15, I'll tell her.

If she comes
at 5:33,
at 5:47,
at 5:59.

Watch the bend in the road.

Then the front door opens,
and Mr. _____'s wife is on the step,
wearing a dress that's green as reeds,
waving her arm.

"Would you like to wait inside?" she asks.

She's trying not to sound like what she's really saying is:
"Where is your mother? Why is she so late to pick you up?"

I wish and I wish, a wish like gritted teeth, to hear Mamma's car, to see it shining around the bend, kicking back the evening light.

I look away from the house, and the wife, and the step.

Look down the path. "I'm okay. Thank you."

She's still standing there when I hear Mamma's car.

"I have to go," I tell her.

I don't look back. Don't wave.

Afterwards. At home. At night. I can't stop picturing her.

I picture her
in front of the mirrored cupboards
in their bedroom,
in that bedroom they sleep in together.
I picture her slicing carrots.
I picture them
sitting in the dining room,
eating dinner,
talking about their days.

Normal things.

He does normal things before he sees me.
He does normal things. After he sees me.

I type:

Can you talk now?

Erase it.

Type:

Sabine, there's something

Erase it.

Type:

Hi

Erase it.

I'm trying to practice piano.

Take a breath. Fingers poised. Start to play.

And the music takes the nothing

and shakes it up like a fizzy drink,

disturbs its shapeless shaping, ruffles, rumples,

goes into me and moves through. Stick insects cover the keys.

Coloring everything, falling like handfuls of dropped pins.

Blue stick insects, darker than before,

dark and darkest blue. Blue of midnight. Blue of ink.

That blue seeps into me as they crawl over my hands,

and the feeling soaks through like cold water.

They multiply, multiply, appearing out of nothing

like they're trying to tell me something.

That just because you don't feel something.

Just because you don't notice something.

Doesn't mean it's not there.

It starts to happen
every time I play,
any time I try to sing.

Throat closed,
chest tight,
hands shaking,
blue, bluest.

Walking across my throat.

The blue changes.

Sometimes it's lighter.
Other times, darker.

Sometimes the stick insects are thick, scraping across keys like pencils.
Other times, they are light and soundless as eyelashes.

There are a thousand kinds of sadness.
A thousand kinds of blue stick insects.

But every time they come.
No matter their shape or shade.
Every time they come, they fill me
with what is unbearable.

For as long as I can remember, I have heard music everywhere.

Sometimes, even in the dank school bathroom,
the extractor fan sounds like it's humming.

I give music to everything—to trees, to the wind, to the toaster.
To footsteps and cars and hinges.

So when I hear the opening strings from "Jóga,"
my favorite Björk song,
when I hear it while I'm walking across
an empty quad at break,
I almost think it's coming from inside my head.

But I follow
the sound
like a path,
find the boy
at the end of it.

The new kid.

He's playing the song on his phone,
holding it out towards a girl
with crossed arms.
"You seriously don't know this?" he says, smiling.
She shakes her head.
Tucks her hair behind her ear.

I tell myself I can look at them for three seconds.

Longer than that and they'll notice.

But the boy turns his head as I'm about to walk away.

"Nell, right?" he says.

Burning eyes.

"You know this song."

He says it like he can see it on my face.

I almost smile.

"Those strings, huh?"

He rolls his eyes like he can't believe it.

"I read
that she does
all the arrangements
herself,
records them
with her voice."

The words are so quiet,
coming out of my mouth.

He catches them. Like loose feathers.

"A Björk fan." His smile softens.

And we don't notice
till ten seconds later:

the other girl
has walked away.

Mora is on new medication.

When we visit her,
I am not the only one who is invisible.

We. Mamma and I. We are both invisible now.

Mora stares past us.

Her eyes go through the wall,
over the city,
over the trees,
all the way to the freezing
summer sea.

She scowls at us,
like we have dragged the world
into the room
on frayed rope.

I am used to this.

Mamma isn't.

On the way home from the clinic, Mamma cries silently,
her fingers trembling as they tap the steering wheel.

As she cries, her face gets younger and younger.

"She ignored me. She just ignored me. Did you see that?"

"Doesn't she know that I'm her mother."

"Doesn't she know who I am."

"Doesn't she know that I raised her."

"They had to cut me open to get her out of me."

"Did you know that? Doesn't she know that?"

I put a hand on Mamma's shoulder. Hold my breath.

I don't want any wings to come out of me, any trailing legs or sticky shells.

I don't want to suddenly feel
whatever it is I didn't know I was feeling.

But I can only hold my breath for forty-three seconds until I give up.
So I wind the window down. Just in case.

Sometimes, when I want to be reminded of peace,
I go to Ouma's house.

It's always quiet there. Always tidy.

She cares for it as if it is a part of her body,
as if it is her body, every surface, every view,
every patch of light a part of her she tends.

But even that, sometimes, is a burden—is too much.
All the windows and every door, every plant and clear, cream wall,
every painting and every book on every shelf.

On those days, she walks in the garden.

"The only thing that heals me, really, is the green."
Walks down a path of mossy stones fanned by strelitzias.

At the bottom of the garden, shaded by rampant ferns,
there is a pond filled with small fish,
moving under jade water like flakes of goldleaf.

She used to worry, when we were little, that we would drown in it.
She used to say, "Don't play by the pond without your ouma, all right?"

One day I said, "But, Ouma, it's shallow. I can't drown in it."
The water only came up to my shins.

She shook her head slowly. Her eyes were very blue.
"Nell," she said. "You can drown in a teaspoon of water."

I pictured myself shrunk down, swimming in a spoon, flailing.
I didn't understand.

She meant, of course,
that human lungs
are not built to tolerate
even a teaspoon of water.
Breathe in a single drop
and you could choke.

But I think she meant something else, too.

Some people drown
all at once,
in oceans,
cold sucking them
towards the sun.

And others drown slowly,
in increments as insignificant
as drops of fresh dew.

Sabine's name lights up my screen.

It would be so easy.
If she were in the room.

I would sit on the end of my bed.
I would sit with her for a little while.

She would know everything.
I wouldn't even have to speak.

I could just tell her to come home for a bit.

Maybe she would listen.

But I don't pick up.

Maybe.
A few weeks ago.
I would have been able to do it.

I would have been able to ask her to come and visit.

But my secrets are like organs now.
Unnecessary hearts. Beating inside me.
Growing and pulsing.
They are rotten. Swollen.
And if I ripped them out of me.
I don't know. If I would survive.

I pick the boy who waved
because he's taller than me.

Because I can see
his brown back,
the lines of his shoulder blades
through his white shirt.

I pick him because he's new.
Because he wasn't around last year.

I pick him because he's in Grade 11.

On the day I pick him,
he's laughing too loudly for the laugh to be real,
talking like he's not the new kid,
like they know him,
like they've always known him.

I walk up to him. Take his hand.
Pull him down the passage.

"Aren't you going to class?" he asks.
Laughing again. Nervous.
I say: "I need to go outside. Come with me?"

The quad is deserted.
There are cracks in the concrete,
weeds growing out of them.
I push the boy against the wall.

Stand on my tiptoes and kiss him.

When I pull away,
there are three
velvet-black butterflies,
wide-winged,
hovering above me.

I watch them. Honey-and-butter
hunger unfurls in my chest.

The boy isn't looking at the butterflies.
He's looking at me.

"Why did you do that?" he asks.

"Just wanted to kiss you," I say.

He doesn't know what to do with this.
Opens his hands and closes them.

The bell rings.

"Come to my house. Tomorrow. After school," I say.

"Are you serious?"

I nod,
but he's already pulling out his phone
to give me his number.

PART THREE

THIRTY-ONE DAYS AFTER THE WASPS

When Mamma is young,
I take the boy to my room.

Mamma doesn't care
if my door is closed.

She's upstairs, staring at her face in the mirror.
She's listening to music and crying. She's a heap under a duvet.

When Mamma is young,
I take the boy to my room
and I let his hands open and
close me. Like I am a hall of clear windows.

I let him kiss me for hours,
let him push his tongue into my mouth.
I let him put his hands up my skirt.

Black-velvet butterflies fill my room,
and when my eyes are open, I watch them,
and I let the wanting fill me.

The boy watches the butterflies, too,
but he hasn't said anything about them.

When he sees them,
it just makes him kiss me more.

The feeling is still mine—
his feelings aren't insects; his are inside him,
invisibles caught in invisible nets,
but seeing them means he gets to see
a secret part of me
made visible with wings.

I have him saved in my phone as *antidote.*

When Mamma is older, when she's downstairs,
when she's sitting in the living room
reading a book, when she's making an early dinner,
when we can't go to my room,

I take the boy's hand and I say we're going for a walk.

I kiss him in the greenbelt behind our house.
I kiss him in the park, sitting on top of the shining slide.
I kiss him in the garage. Leaving trails of dancing shadow.

I kiss him, listening to music in Mamma's parked car,
wearing out the battery. I kiss him
until black butterflies cover the windshield,
until they block out all the day's old light.

"You haven't told me anything about you," the boy says
one day when we're sitting in Mamma's car. No black butterflies yet.
He raises his eyebrows. "Like, what do you like doing?"

"This," I say. But he pushes me off softly. "Okay. I sing."

I can tell he knows it's something true.

"Sing me something?"
"No. Sorry."
"Please?"
"I have to go."

I find myself getting out of the car.
I find myself walking away from him.
Turning my back on him. I do it so easily.

I can't tell him
he's not the antidote
if he's talking to me
about music.

Music makes the stick insects come.
Sharp ends. Throat-tickling feet.

Music brings on the wasps. Music reminds me of beetles.

I can't tell him the truth so I let him go on
thinking that I'm shallow, that all I want is the kissing.

He keeps coming back, though.
To open all the windows, and to close them.

And when he does.
I am all glass, all clouds reflected.

I am a long passage of sun-caught mirrors,
black wings as far as the eye can see.

The next time I go to a music lesson,
there's a sticky beetle on the back of my neck.
Peel it off and look at it, sitting in my hand.
Shame burrows into me, down my throat, under my skin.
I wait until it dies—wait until the feeling dies—
and then I throw the beetle in the bushes,
wipe my hands on my skirt as I walk up the brick path
to the front door. I decide: I won't eat until tomorrow.

A few days
before Mora
went to the clinic,
she was up late,
music making
her bedroom
door rattle.

I couldn't sleep all night,
listening to the rattling.
But I was scared.

Too scared to go to her room.

The next morning,
there were pages pinned
to the laundry line.

Thick pages from a sketchbook.
Torn out. Ragged and reddish brown.
Kicked in the wind like stiff pillowcases.

It was one of those crisp, vivid mornings. No rain.
The sun closer to white than yellow.

I walked up to the line, to see the pages closer.
I tapped one with my finger.

Smell of iron.

The pages. They weren't covered with paint.
They were painted, every one of them, with blood.

That's when Mamma and Dad started to see.
Those pieces of paper like flags.

Not flags of surrender. Declarations of war.

There were other moments.

Mora standing in front of a mirror,
putting a belt around her neck and pulling it
tighter and tighter.
Blood dripping from her arms.
The music like loose electricity.

I was the one who found her.

And there was the time I saw her sitting
at the bottom of the garden,
burning the inside of her forearm
with a cigarette.

My sister has circles and circles
going up and down her arms.
Circles like little stop signs. Little buttons.
Stop/Go. Off/On.

Sometimes I think
Mamma and Dad
don't want to hear
what is most loud.

Don't want to see
what is
most obvious.

It would
pull them under
if they
admitted it.

If they saw how bad it really was.

So they keep their eyes covered.
They're always turning the other way.
Or else they're staring Mora in the face
like she is a blank wall, an inaudible signal.

Thinking about Mora,
remembering her—the beginning and the endless middle—

and I'm alone at home, without the boy, without anyone,
Dad at work, Mamma at the clinic,

and I'm lying on my bed and it just happens.
They just—happen.

Wasps.

Pressing down around me like an asthma attack,
black-green and glossy,
iridescent as oil on water, swirling,
tunnel of wings and sound.

I turn my face away,
but my eyes are drawn back to them.

Can't stop watching them.

The feeling pours into me. Scalding.
Anger that makes my hands shake. Anger that will devour me.

I have no choice but to stare into the swarm.
No choice but to feel it.

After I sweep away the wasps,
throw them outside on the summer-dry lawn,

I message the boy:

What are you doing tonight?

Nothing. Homework. Why?

Can I come over?

Now?

Now

Okay

I could've invited him to my house,
like I always do.
But I want to leave. I want to go somewhere.
Walk somewhere. In the dark.
I need to move.

So I go to his house. For the first time.

His parents aren't there. Neither is his older brother.

He makes me tea,
tea with milk and two sugars,
but I don't drink it.

I walk up to him,
tugging at his hands.

Sit on the kitchen counter.
Put my legs around him.

He makes a noise like he's angry,
sad, hungry, and I kiss him, let him kiss me.

Black butterflies all around us and I
drink them in with my eyes,
feel the night-warmth of wanting.

When the black butterflies arrive,
I forget that a single wasp has ever existed.
I forget about the color blue.

The next morning,
I walk to school early,
before the earth is awake.

Blue morning, like all it can remember is night.

The rain sits in the air
without letting go.

Occasionally a car rushes by,
making music of puddles.

Get to the school gates,
walk slower.
The price of entering
is heaviness.

The school is still empty,
the hallways full of the night's silence.
It's peaceful, almost.

Then, in a gray, deserted passage, I see the boy.
The low ceiling lifts a little.

He strides towards me, almost running.
His arms are open and he sweeps me into them.

We are all alone.

My cheek lands
comfortably
in the hollow
where his chest
meets his shoulder.

"Hey," he says.

"Hey."

We separate,
air between us.

And then the space is filled
with pale-pink butterflies,
golden at the edges,
rippling in the dim light.

Pink butterflies. Gold, orange, fuchsia.

When I watch them,
I can feel all those colors inside me:

spring evenings,
sweet-sour apples,
blushing.

The boy laughs softly.
"Nell—all the butterflies—are they?"
"They're mine," I say.

He looks at me like he's fine with this.
Doesn't try to understand.
He's happy to watch them with me.

It feels strange,
almost too close,
him watching my magic
and believing it instantly,
without question.

We watch the butterflies flying past closed doors,
past little windows, past lockers, past the principal's office.

We watch them
and he doesn't look away—not once.

I don't look away either.

I let
all of it
fill me.

I go to Mr. _____'s side.

His arm around my waist again.

He pulls me onto his lap.

The same old static.

He smells like peppermint chewing gum.

His jersey is scratchy

against the curve of my bare arm.

"Now," he says, patting the tops of my thighs. "Did you practice this week?"

I nod silently, turning my face to the piano.

White keys. Black keys. Brown wood.

I know I'm making it awkward, staying quiet, but I can't help it.

All the words I could say. Want to say. All the words he wants me to say.

They are stuck to the one word I cannot say.

So his hands rest on my thighs.

My back is against his chest. His cheek close to my cheek.

"Okay, you can begin with your scales," he says. Shifts in his chair.

Released, I move towards the piano,

scanning the carpet for sticky beetles, looking for wasps.

"What is it?" he says. "Is there a fly in the room again?"

Shake my head like punctuation.

Sit down and play. Loud.

Like closing your eyes and talking over
the worst scene in a movie.

Thursday, and I pass a girl who says,

"Your sister is a freak."

I don't want to look at her

blazer pinned with badges,

her greasy middle parting.

I walk straight to the boy

and I take his hand

and I lead him to the girls' bathroom.

The graffiti on the tiled wall says

Mora Strand gives good head.

The bathroom is filled with wings as soon as we start kissing,

and I am unbuttoning my dress to feel his hands against my skin.

"Nell," he says, "why did Mina Tredoux

call your sister a freak?" The black butterflies fall,

dying instantly, lying on the ground like litter.

"I mean, I've heard from other people—

stories about your sister. But—are the stories true?"

I want to say that they are true. Most of them, anyway.

I want to say that doesn't give anyone the right to call my sister a freak.

But all I say is: "It's stupid. Mina Tredoux is stupid."

I don't want to talk about Mora. I want the black butterflies back.

But the boy is looking at me like he's worried.

"Mora's got issues," I say. "Mental health stuff."

"That must be really hard." Takes my hand.

"I have to go," I say, stepping over the dead butterflies.

"Wait. Nell."

But I don't turn back.

We're in the TV room at the boy's house,
watching a movie,
when his older brother,
Cole, comes in.
I guess I've been over a lot
because he looks at me
and says, "You again."
The boy squirms on the couch.

Cole is standing in the door,
leaning against the frame, eating biltong.

He's nineteen. It's like he lives in another country.

He's at university, and he has a car,
and he's in a band that actually plays gigs.

He stands there, staring.

"What?" says the boy.
"Nothing, nothing," says Cole.
He turns to leave, then looks back at me.
"You know you're too pretty for him, right?"
The boy clears his throat.
"I'm serious," says Cole, looking at him hard.
"Way out of your league."

Later, when Mamma messages me to say she's outside,
the boy says, "Sorry about earlier."

"It's not your fault."
"No—the thing is—"
"He's your brother. I get it."

I hug him, pressing my face into his shoulder.

"For the record. I don't think I'm out of your league."
"Oh." He laughs. "You are. But thank you."
"I kissed you, remember?"
"I'm still not sure why you did that." Smiling.

I did it because I have wings inside me.
And when they come. I have to feel things.
I have to feel things I don't want to feel.

"Just wanted to, I guess."
"Were you upset? It was almost like—
like you were having a panic attack or something.
Did something happen that day?"
"Nothing happened," I tell him.

When I get into Mamma's car,
I think maybe she's going to ask who the boy is.
If he's my boyfriend.

Because
she's been dropping me off
at his house
a lot.

But she's seventeen today,
so she doesn't say anything.

Just touches my hair,
air-kisses me,
turns the music up loud.

The whole time.

The whole time I'm in Mr. _____'s study.

I can hear his wife.

Walking up and down.

This is the first time I've been able to hear her like this.

So persistently. Even though the door is still closed.

I imagine walking through the house. Going to find her.

I imagine watching her from behind, her slow,

calm movements slowing me, calming me.

I imagine sitting at the small round table in her kitchen,

sitting down and looking at her shoulders under her cardigan

as she turns the kettle on for tea. I imagine finding her,

finding her, finding her. Finding her, and she doesn't look up at me.

In the dining room, folding napkins.

In the TV room, watching some show about gardens or antiques.

In the bathroom, touching up her lipstick. Dabbing concealer under her eyes.

But even though I can imagine finding her.

Looking at her.

I can't imagine her looking back at me.

I can't imagine what I would say. Can't imagine speaking.

Even if I tried. I know. Nothing would come out.

My mouth would open. White noise would fill the room.

I've started coughing them up.

In the middle of the night, I wake with a weight on my chest,
like someone has put the moon there for safekeeping.

Solid rock. Immovable.

I press my palms into the mattress and I try to breathe.
The weight lifts and then the coughing starts.

I cough green-dark wasps into my hands, each one slimed with saliva.
I cough up blue stick insects, fat as cigars.

I hold them in my palms. I watch them twitch until they die.

When I cough up the wasps and the stick insects,
the feelings are softer, briefer, less alive.

Even if my throat burns,
it's better than wings
glossing the air without warning.

I guess the apples and the antidote
are working. Even if the wings still come.
Even if they won't stop coming.

I cough the wasps and the stick insects up,
and then I bury them
in my mother's beautiful garden.

Sabine calls. "Haven't heard from you in ages," she says.
"And Ouma tells me you haven't been to visit for a while."

She doesn't want to admit that she's asking questions.

Are you okay?
Is everything all right?

"I've been busy," I tell her.
"How's school going?"
"I don't like it."
"The teachers?"
"I don't like anything about it."

Except—

"Haven't you met anyone interesting?"

I can tell she can see I'm thinking of someone.

"Okay, there's a boy—"
"A boy." This makes her happy.

Straight away, though, I think about the girls' bathroom.
Grubby tiles. Graffiti. My lips hot and numb. I think about the boy's hands.
His face is a blur to me. He wears a mask of black butterflies.

"It's nothing, though. We just keep each other company."
"Company is good. You been writing in your notebook?"

I shake my head. No use in lying.

"Nope. Been too busy with school. Practicing and stuff."

The lie tastes like ivory. Piano keys. Sweat.

Sabine looks a little sad. "Are you sure everything's okay, Nell?"
She's looking at me through the screen, squinting a little,
like she wishes her hair could tell her my secrets.

"Everything's fine," I hear myself say. "I have to go."
"Okay. Call me if you need anything. You can call me anytime."

People always say stuff like that.

You can call me anytime.
Shout if you need anything.

If I actually shouted.
I wonder what would happen.

If I actually shouted.
It would be more like a scream.

If I actually shouted.
I would never stop shouting.

Mr. ____'s hands don't make the black butterflies appear.
They're not like the boy's.

When his hand is on my thigh, nothing happens.
No wings—not anymore. Not even wasps.

Even when I am alone,
they don't rise into the air.

When I am alone, I cough them out. Burn and bile.

On the nights after I have had a music lesson, I cough for hours.
Line the slick bodies up, scrape them into the bin when I'm done.

Here's where I exist.

Between.

I want someone to look at me.

Really look at me.

And as soon as someone looks at me.

I want them to look away.

"So, do you write songs?"

I've never told the boy that I write songs.
I've never told anyone except Sabine.

I keep them secret,
sing quietly in my room,
even though I wish someone would knock on the door—
Mamma, Dad, anyone,
some stranger from down the road—
and say, "That sounds so good. What is that? Did you write that?"

I pull a face. "What? No. Who told you that?"
Those last words are softer than I want them to be.

"No one. But you sing, you play piano—I mean. I thought maybe . . ."

The boy is peeling a naartjie carefully and I am watching his hands.
He has beautiful hands, long fingers,
the shells of his pink nails light against warm brown skin.

He has hands that make things, remake things.
He makes me. Remakes me under them like I am damp sand.
And I have never asked him a single question about him.
Haven't asked him, once, what he does with his hands when I'm not around.

It was cruel. Saving his name in my phone as *antidote*. Like he's a thing.
I'd never want someone to do that to me. But I did it to him.

The thing about the boy is, he's totally unaffected by everything—
the noise in the quad, the sun beating down, the bell ringing.
I want to reach inside him and pull out whatever cool river flows there.
Drink from it like a mountain stream.

"Hello?" He laughs. "Where'd you go?"
He puts a naartjie segment in his mouth. Whole. "Want some?" he asks.
But I shake my head and kiss him until
a black butterfly sits on my chest like a locket.

Afterwards, because I'm feeling guilty,
I ask him what he does with his hands.
When I'm not around.

"That's a weird way of putting it." He laughs.
"You know what I mean."
"Okay. Uh. I play guitar."

For a second, I can picture it:
the boy playing guitar, me singing. Together.

"I have a band," he says. "I mean—my brother has a real band.
They play shows and stuff. I just have a, you know.
It's just a thing I do with my friends."

He has a band. Of course he has a band. With his friends. His new friends.
I'm the only person who sings secretly.
Other people. Normal people. They have bands. They have friends.

When he says: "I have a band,"
I hear: "I already have people to play music with.
And you won't even sing in front of me. Remember?"

"Who's in the band?" I ask.
"Just some guys. We're not good or anything."
"I bet you are."
"My brother's better."
Then, like one of those wasps coughed out, I say, "I'm good."
He smiles.
"What?" I'm laughing.

"I know you are."

"You've never even heard me—"

"You just look like the kind of girl . . ."

"Kind of girl . . ."

"Who's good at everything."

"I'm good at this," I say. And I kiss him.

His fingertips on my neck

and I am floating

into a sky of shimmering wings.

I have a rule:
I can eat anything as long as it fits in the palm of my hand.

Things that fit in the palm of my hand:
a single apple,
a square of chocolate,
a dried peach.

The other rule I have is: say no to everything.

At school, the boy is always offering:
bite of my pie,
sip of my juice,
a Coke,
a strip of guava roll.

No, no thanks, no thank you.
No, I'm fine. Nope, not hungry.

It tastes good, the word *no.*
It feels good to say it.

That word. It comes out of my mouth. But it's nourishing to me.
It sits in the pit of my stomach, as rich as a knuckle of butter.

There are places I can't say no.
Places where no doesn't work.

I can't say no to Mr. ＿＿＿.

All I say is yes.

Yes silently. Yes with my body.

I've been saying yes for so long.

No wonder he thinks
he always has permission
to touch me.

Touches me on the back of my neck,
rubbing his thumb against a freckle.

He pats his lap, and I sit there,
I sit on his lap like a dog.

I don't say no. I never say it.

There are some things. This is what this room has taught me.
There are some things. That words can't do.

The boy's body pressed into mine, his face against my neck.

Dark-velvet butterflies filling the room,
lit with sparkling pink and gold.

The boy is used to the butterflies now.

Whenever they arrive, appearing like new stars,
he watches them for a little while.
The same look he has when he's watching me.

My phone drops out of my pocket.
He picks it up.

There's a message from him on the screen,
a message he sent an hour ago:

outside your house

He knows he sent it, because he knows they're his words
but his name's not there. His name is—

"Antidote?"
He drags the back of his hand across his mouth.
"It's a joke," I say, smoothing my skirt down.
"Antidote to what?"
All the butterflies fall to the floor.
The wanting and the glowing die with them.

I need him to come closer. To put his hands on my cheeks again.

"Antidote to what?"

"It's—you make me feel better."
"I make you feel better."

I squeeze the tips of my fingers, one by one.

"Better about what?"

My head is a montage of blood. Bare hands. Closed doors.
I can hear music. Mora's music. That's all I can hear.

But I can't say any of that. There aren't any words.

The room is filled with flies.

I look at them.
I want to speak.

But all I have
is a throat
of desperate,
nonsensical buzzing.

The boy bats the flies away.

"Nell."

"I can't . . ."

"I don't know anything about you.
I don't know what you like to play on piano.
I don't know which music school you go to.
I don't know who your friends are—
or who your friends used to be."

He looks around my bedroom.

"You don't even have anything on your walls."

He puts his hands on my shoulders.

"Just tell me why you're sad.
We don't have to do stuff all the time.
We could talk."

"I don't want to talk."

He waits there. In front of me. For a little while. The flies whine.

"I think I'm going to go home, then."

Grabs his stuff and leaves.

I watch him walking up the path,
through the garden,
the trees and their red flowers
reaching for him in the wind.

I stare at the path until my eyes go out of focus.
Until the flies turn everything fuzzy.

I don't want to visit Mora.

"Take Dad with you,"
I tell Mamma,
ignoring the fact that she has never,
not once,
taken Dad with her.

"Take Ouma," I say.
"Take someone else."

But she won't hear it.

"You're coming with me," she says.

Mamma is sixteen. She's wearing Mora's clothes.

Mora's baggy cardigan, green as a wet field,
green as the greenbelts rich people ride their horses through.
Mora's jeans, with the extra black stars she sewed on the pockets.
She smells like Mora, and she looks like Mora, and we're going to see Mora,
and Mora's name is the loudest thing in the universe,
a name that holds everything together. Takes everything apart.

"Fine," I say, putting my jacket on.

At the door, Mamma stops on the threshold.
She looks at me. I immediately want her to look away.

"You're so beautiful these days, Nell."

She squeezes my arm and smiles,
like she's proud of this compliment.

And all the way up the path
to the car
I think about
the cost of being visible.

Mora is fine. By Mora standards.
She doesn't say anything about Mamma wearing her clothes.

I'm glad I haven't eaten all day,
because I haven't seen the boy in a week,
haven't even talked to him,
and I really—really—don't want my magic to happen in front of Mora.

My mind leaves the room, goes to the boy.
How he wanted to talk. How I couldn't.

When I come back, Mora is saying,

"I don't want to leave. I like it here."
"But this isn't your home," says Mamma.
"You're coming home?" I ask.

Mamma nods. Mora shakes her head.

"You can't stay here forever, Mora."

I keep trying to picture Mora
back in her room.

But all I can think about
are those pages she tore from her sketchbook,
caked with her own blood.

Mamma makes her hug me goodbye,
and when she's close to me,
I can feel the music under her skin.

When we get home,
we walk back down the path.
Through the drenched garden.

It rained while we were out.
Water drips off the ends of the leaves.
Muddy puddles on the lawn.

And I think about what Ouma said about drowning,
and I know that I am a girl
drowning, teaspoon by teaspoon.

Mora's bedroom window is milk white
with moonlight. Blank as a screen.

Mora got a boyfriend a few months after she got her magic.

His name was Thad.

He looked like a surfer or a skater but he didn't skate or surf—
all he did was talk, and everything that came out of his mouth was stupid.

She was proud of him, though. She liked to show him off.
I guess she wanted me to know she had something I didn't.

"I'm going to Thad's house," Mora told me one Saturday.
"Do you want to come?"

For weeks she had been acting like I didn't exist. So I told her I wanted to go.
I was desperate for any way to know her again. Desperate for her to like me.

Mamma dropped us off.
The whole house was pale brown, inside and out.
Even the lawn was turning brown,
bleached by the rainless summer.

"Are we going to watch a movie or something?"

Thad laughed, and Mora gave me this look,
like she was trying to tell me to stop being such a loser.

They drifted away from me, Thad's laughter
lost somewhere in the house. I heard them close a door.

I walked around,
looking at the blank walls.
There wasn't a single book anywhere.
Not even a cookbook.

In the end, I went outside and sat down on the crunchy lawn.

Hours later, Mora came to find me, leaning against the glass sliding door.
"Can you message Mamma? I ran out of data."

I typed: *Can you come fetch us now? The movie's finished*
"Done," I told Mora.

"Stop sulking," she said, misreading the frown on my face.
"You'll get your own boyfriend eventually."

Most of the time, Mora and Saskia acted like I was invisible.

But then,
some days,
they adopted me.
Like a pet.

One afternoon, Saskia said, "Come out with us."
Mora pulled a face, but when she locked eyes with Saskia,
who was stroking my hair with her fingertips,
she changed the position of her mouth.
"Yeah," she said. "Come out with us."

I didn't believe her,
didn't believe for a second that she actually wanted to invite me,
but I also couldn't resist it: the chance to be her friend for a night.

Even if I knew we were all just pretending.

I let her and Saskia dress me up.

I let them say things like:
"Oh my God, your boobs. Everyone is going to go crazy."
"You're so pretty. I hate you."

They kissed me on the cheeks in front of the mirror,
like they were in an American movie.
With Mora so close to me, I could feel the music under her skin.

My sister, the undercurrent.

Mamma dropped the three of us off at the party.

The house was in one of those suburbs near the train station.
The street was dark, the concrete curb spilling out weeds.

Mamma looked at the shabby house.
One of the windows was cracked. Veins in a glass wrist.
"It's nice you're spending time with your sister,"
she said as I was getting out the car.
But I could see she was worried. Because Mora and Saskia
had dressed me like I was up for auction.
Because all the streetlights were out, the road narrow,
because we could hear the trains moving along their tracks.

Mora was standing on the curb,
pulling out her cigarettes,
lighting one, taking a drag.

Mamma looked at me, hard.
"Look after your sister," she said.
"I'll pick you up at twelve."

I got out the car, wishing I'd brought a jacket,
feeling awkward in my tight top, in Mora's shoes.
I hobbled up the path to the door.

Mora threw herself through that door, shouting,
Saskia already dancing,
and there was so much noise and light,
there were so many bodies.

I lost them immediately.

I moved through packed rooms,
skin goosebumped,
arms folded across my front.

"Oh my God, are you Mora's sister?" someone asked me.

Then I spotted Thad in the corner of the room, talking to Mora.
He let go of her waist and looked straight at me and whistled.
And I didn't want to smile, but I smiled—even though I hated Thad,
even though the whistle went into me like a tightened screw.

The smile came from somewhere else.
From the place in me that had always felt invisible.
The place in me that wanted the heat of being seen.

Mora rolled her eyes.
And even though Thad was across the room
and there was so much music between us, space and light,
his eyes hooked into me like talons.

Outside, in the cold and the dark,
Mora talked to me looking straight ahead.

"Next time,"
she said, "maybe don't dress like that
when Thad's around?"

I turned to Saskia,

but she just stared down the road, silent,

like it had nothing to do with her.

Saskia is different now.

When I pass her in gray passages,
she looks at me, but there's no recognition.

Maybe I am different, too.
But I still look the same.

Saskia, on the other hand—
she wears her blazer every day like a symbol.
She's always neat, her socks pulled up,
the tiny golden studs in her earlobes
shining like medals, her face as clean as a baby's.

Saskia showed up to school this year with her hair cut short—
a pixie cut, like the ones from the nineties. No eyeliner.
She doesn't talk to boys anymore. She's always reading a book.

Around her, there's an electric fence,
ticking with dangerous current.

I don't even try to talk anymore.
I look, and then I look away.

I can't sleep, the night I know
Mora will be coming home.

The piano is closed and I won't look at it.

Then the wasps appear.

This time, I don't cough them up,

one by one.

This time, they fill the room.

I turn my music up. Loud.
So Mamma doesn't hear them.

The wasps fill the room,
diving in lazy arcs, charcoal vapor.

I watch them.

The anger
pulls me to standing,
pulls my voice out of my throat,
ragged noise, pinched screaming.

Try to cover my eyes,
but I keep dropping my hands.

I have to look at them.

Then I hear something.

Not something—inside me.
Not something—that came from me.
Something outside.
A sound like a dropped bag of stones.

And even though I don't know what it is—
what made the sound—
I know it's the sound of disaster.

When you have lived in a house
where around every corner
there could be a puddle of blood,
you learn to listen out for it:
the sound of something terrible.

This sound—whatever it is—
reminds me of that.

The wasps die instantly,
die all at once, falling to the floor.

The room is filled with ants then,
ants the color of blood
and ants the color of steel,
ants moving like iron filings
up and down the walls,
writhing, a living surface.

Big-bodied ants, fat and glossy,
a carpet of them
covering the floorboards.

I was wondering. When I would see.
What fear looked like.

There are ants in my hair when I walk outside.
I can feel one crawling on my temple.

Ants stream alongside me in tributaries as I step into the dark of the garden.

Mamma is lying on the bricks,
small and crumpled.
Barely twenty.

She was the sound.
The dropped bag of stones.
It was the sound of her falling.

And some part of me knew it—
knew the sound
of someone trying to die.

I want to whisper. Want to say something. I don't speak.

Dad's woken up, too.
He's at the door.
Then he's beside her.
Barefoot blur.

He's talking to her.
He doesn't have ants in his hair.
His throat hasn't closed up.

"I'm fine," Mamma is saying when I walk closer, each step careful.
"I'm fine. I just need a cup of tea."

That's when I see the blood.
Trickling down the back of her neck, soaking her hair.

"I'm taking you to the hospital," says Dad.

Mamma leans against him for a little bit before her legs give way.

I open my mouth again, but it's empty.

"Nell. Go inside. Go to sleep," says Dad.

Ants around my wrists like bracelets.

Mamma is so young,
so small in Dad's arms.

He walks up the pathway,
carrying her.

I hear the car door close,
and then he comes back for the keys.

"Go to sleep," he says again.
Quickly, he touches my head.

I go inside, where the ants are still dripping down the walls like toxic damp.
I sit on the end of my bed, breathing staccato, until they die.
Watch their little bodies falling out of my hair.

When I go back to feeling nothing, I fetch the broom
and sweep the wasps up, sweep away the ants.

I get into bed.

I sleep like I've swallowed the mountain.

The best memories I have of Mamma
are all the ordinary days
she made into special occasions.

One night, when she was thirty-seven,
she called us inside early,
when the light was beginning to dip.

She had made a nest—
duvets and blankets and pillows
on the carpet
in the TV room.

She got us to lie down.
She covered us with blankets.
And then she walked through the house,
turning off all the lights.

The darkness wrapped us up.
I could hear her moving in it.

"Mamma?" I said. "What are you doing?"
"Shhh," she said. "Just listen."

Music started to play.

"It's the best way to listen to a song," she whispered to us.
"So you can hear every note. Every syllable."

I lay there, and even though I was usually scared
of everything I couldn't see,
I wasn't afraid. I was listening to Tori Amos's voice,
listening to my mother in the dark.

When it ended, Mamma turned the lights back on.

The darkness and the song had gone into me.

"What was the point of that?" Mora barked, sitting up.
She rubbed at her eyes. "That was so stupid."

"I liked it, Mamma," I said.

I wanted to say it again.

But I could see something had changed in Mamma.

And then she was in the kitchen,
her face smooth, suddenly younger,
much younger, suddenly eighteen,
making dinner, boiling water for pasta,

pretending

the darkness—
the nest—
the song—

hadn't even happened.

What happens in my family: a disaster, then a vacuum.

We go to our own rooms to think about what happened.

What was done. What wasn't done. We don't talk about it afterwards.

Dad doesn't come home from the emergency room and say, "Are you okay?"

He makes coffee and goes to work.

And I want to call Ouma, but I don't know how to speak against the silence.

In bed, Mamma is twenty-three,
drinking carrot juice.
"They said I have to rest."

She's got stitches on the back of her head. "I'm glad you're okay, Mamma."

She bats at the white sheets. "I'm fine. I just slipped."

"What were you doing on the roof?"

"I wanted to look at the stars."

The words don't sit right against each other.

"Stars?" I say.

"I was having a moment, I don't know. It was stupid."

"Mamma. You could have died."

"But I didn't."

She takes
another sip
of her juice.

"Don't you have to go to school?"

At school, I walk through forests of elbows and shoulders,
crowds of blue jerseys with heads attached to them, mouths moving.

The boy is there. He's talking to his friends.
He's one of the moving mouths. He looks at me. For a moment.
Then he looks away.

Then he's running up behind me:
"Nell. I'm sorry. About the other day."

My relief is a wash of white damselflies, dancing, translucent, to the ground.
I watch them, the cool rush of their light rinsing me.

He watches them, too. Smiles a soft smile.
"Do you want to come to a show later?
My brother's band. They're playing a gig in town."

My answer:
one burning kiss.

They pick me up later that evening.

Dad's at work late, and Mamma's at the clinic,
so I don't even have to ask if I can go out.

Sit in the back seat next to the boy,
knees touching,
my shoulder pressed against his arm.

The boy introduces me to the other guys
in his brother's band—Khaya and Avi.

Cole puts music on, and it's loud, so no one tries to talk over it.
The sound sinks into me like teeth.

It's trip-hop, I think. Tremolo wavering like double vision,
a woman's voice like concentrated moonlight.

The boy, whispering close to my ear: "Her voice is so cool."

A praying mantis appears, sitting on the back of Khaya's headrest,
a stalk of lime green. It turns its head to look at me.

I am jagged with envy.

"Is that?" says the boy.

I nod, hiding my face.

"Hey, it's okay." Putting his arms around me.

When I look at the praying mantis again, it dies, falling at my feet.
I pick it up, open the window, toss it away, glad to be numb.

We wind past the University of Cape Town,
its windows clinging to the last of the sun.

When I was little,
I used to think UCT
was a mansion;
a castle on a hill.
I used to think
I could live there one day,
used to think
I'd be happy in a house
with so many windows,
each holding their own
palmful of light.

"So, Nell—what exactly do you see in my brother?"
Cole locks eyes with me in the rearview mirror.

He laughs, and Khaya and Avi laugh, too.
I guess it's the kind of joke brothers make.

But when I glance at the boy, I can tell he's not a part of it.

"Finally got a girl to look at you for longer than two seconds, huh?"
Cole finds my eyes again. "Just don't give it up too fast.
Or he'll be in love with you forever."

More laughter, then the music is loud again.

I slide my hand into the boy's hand and squeeze it.

On the floor of Cole's car, under my feet, there is a magazine.
The woman on the cover is wearing bikini bottoms,
holding her arm across her breasts to cover her nipples.

When we get to Long Street,
and Cole parallel parks without batting an eye,
we climb out of the car and the streets are glistening
with the spattered shine of blue rain.

The sun is sinking, casting a spotlight down the road.

Inside the small, dark-windowed bar, the band starts setting up.

"Sorry about—about what he said. In the car," says the boy.
"He can be an asshole."

There's static coming from the stage, then feedback,
loud enough to feel like needles.

The boy's hands cover my ears.
He cringes at the sound.

"He was just joking around," I shout. "It's fine."

But something has worn away between us.

I touch his shoulder. "He shouldn't have embarrassed you like that."
"That's what he does," the boy says.

Then the bar starts to fill up, and the music starts,
Cole fronting the band, playing guitar,
singing into the mic, and we can't talk anymore.

The boy turns to the bartender and gets me a Coke,
and I drink it slowly,
letting the distortion crowd my chest.

It feels a lot like the numbness, like nothing,
that staticky sound, like a swallowed howl.

The boy doesn't take my hand.
We're both staring at his brother.

Outside,

on the curb,

Khaya and Avi

load their gear

back into the car.

The boy's gone

to the bathroom,

and Cole is

standing next to me,

on the pavement,

watching his friends

do all the work.

"Want some?" he says.

Hands me a glass

he's carried outside

from the bar.

There's a little

bit of liquid left in it,

watered down

with melted ice.

"SoCo and lime."

I don't know why,

but I take a sip.

I can't look

into his eyes.

I'm thinking about

how he stood up

on that little stage,

in the corner

of the dingy bar,

singing like
he didn't care.
I'm thinking about
the way he moves
when he's playing
guitar, how he ran
one hand
through his hair
when he stopped
to take a sip of water.
"You're a good singer," I say.
He considers me.
"Thanks," he says,
climbing into the car
and hooting.
"What's taking you so long!" he shouts.
Then the boy appears
in the doorway.
"Hey," he says.
"Hey," I say.
He's shy now, embarrassed,
like standing next to
his brother takes
that still, cold stream
at his center
and turns it into
a tepid puddle.
In the car,
instead of looking
at the boy,

I look out the window.

But I can feel

his hot arm

against my arm.

I rest my head

on his shoulder.

When I open my eyes,

the car is idling

outside my house,

and there are

pink-golden butterflies

in the air.

"What the hell, man?" says Cole,

swatting them away.

Khaya is taking a video.

Avi is passed out.

"We're here," says the boy,

softly, in my ear. "I'll walk you in."

He's looking at the butterflies

like they're miraculous.

It's the same way he looks at me.

"Sorry that was so awkward," he says.

We're standing in the garden.

All the lights in the house are off,
meaning Mamma and Dad have gone to sleep.

"No, it's fine, it's—boys, you know.
When they're together."
"My brother can be—"
"It's fine," I tell the boy. "It's really fine."

But something has begun.

It started with the praying mantis,
and it continued with the distortion,
with Cole's voice,
and it didn't end when he handed me
that glass of SoCo and lime.

When I told him he was a good singer.
When he looked back at me.

Cole hoots, then we hear the car screeching off.

"Kiss me," I tell the boy, and he does,
and I pull him inside, through the dark house,
to my bedroom. We lie on my bed.

His hands under my shirt,
his fingertips pressing into my rib cage,
and there are no wasps,
only giant, black-velvet butterflies,
skirting the ceiling, flying high and slow.

I watch them,
full of the hungering,
the wanting

that pushes
every other
possible feeling
away.

Singing days are the worst days.

Just the thought of that small room.
Rough blue carpet and the barred window
that looks out onto the garden.
The pressure inside me alters.
Like opening a car door at a hundred kilometers an hour.

Step inside the house.
Hear the piano down the passage.
Follow the sound.

The doorway appears
like a spoken question
and I am through it
without thinking how to reply.

The next day,
at school,
it feels like I've swallowed
an ocean's worth of fog.
The day drags light behind it
like a packed trailer.
My bones are heavy as grandfather clocks
and my head burns, relentless.

It's not that anything happened.
It's that—everything happened.
Everything is happening and it's too much for me.

Sometimes I forget.
And then something comes loose.
All the screws clatter.
I'm on my knees, feeling in the dirt for lost parts.

The only thing I can think to do is walk across
the field at break.

All the way to the fence.

I just want to get as far away
from the building as possible.

The quad.
The bathroom stalls.
Chilly passages.
Blackboards and chalk.

The desks lined up in rows.

Every surface rings with death.
My sister haunts the staircases.

On the damp field,
the wind comes up behind me,
holds me for a moment,
and then it feels like the wind is going through me,
and the traffic hushes by through the rain,
and I see the gray moths.

They are not the same as the first time.
They are darker now, their wings heavy,
fluffy, thick as dust,
antennae long and feathered.

They flutter up and around me, over me.
They clot the sky with their wings.

I've looked up too fast.
The ground surges up to meet me like a wave.
My mouth full of grass.

The gray moths float over me, silking my cheeks with their wings.
The feeling pushes into me. Heaviness. Hopelessness.

An always feeling of never-change.

"You collapsed," someone says when I wake up in the sick room.

I'm blinking, but I can't see much. The room is full of dotted light.

"Nell.
Nell Strand.
That's your name, isn't it?
Have you eaten anything today?
You look pale."

I shake my head.

"No, you haven't eaten?"

I shake my head again.

"Here. Have some juice. Some sugar will sort you out."

"I don't want juice."

I am handed the juice anyway.

"We've tried calling your mum.
But she's not answering.
Do you have another number?"

The numbers that lead to Dad. They lurch into my mind.

When I say them out loud. It's like I'm saying a spell.

Dad's car. I climb into the passenger seat.

"Are you sick?" he says,
and I don't know
if he's irritated,
impatient, stressed out,
anxious, or angry
because in Dad's voice
they all sound the same.

"I don't know. Probably just tired."

We drive home in silence.

The world slides by,
house by house, door by door,
window by window,
and it seems like every house,
every door, every window—
clean and brightly painted—
is saying the same thing:
you will never feel safe again.

At school, there are dead moths everywhere.
The wind takes them, lifts them, carries them through the air.

They fall in the quad
when the air settles.
They float through windows
and land on desks.
They fall on the grass.
They fall on the bricks,
on tar, on concrete.
They fall on stone.
On the roots of trees.

When they land, they are so light they don't disturb anything.

They will be swept away this evening.
Tomorrow morning, they will be gone.

After Dad drops me at home, I eat a muffin.
Eat it fast, so I can't change my mind.
I don't even enjoy it. I tear it apart, stuff fingerfuls
into my mouth. There's something defiant in me,
a voice that speaks slowly and calmly, that says:

You are not Mora in a pool of blood.
You are not Mamma in a heap on the bricks.
You want to live. You want to live.

I eat the muffin, a handful of wasps coursing around me.
Watch them, feel the neon-buzz of anger.

I do want to live.
I don't want to faint in fields,
covered, eyelid to ankle,
with gray moths. I want to live.

I finish the muffin, watch the handful of wasps until they die.

Then I pick them up, throw them out the kitchen window,
and as I let them drop out of my hands, I hear myself whispering thank you.

Mamma is upstairs, sleeping,
her bedroom door a little open.

I go to my room.
My room. With its blank walls.

I lie on my back and close my eyes.
Comfort myself by talking in a steady voice.
In this voice I say, hold on now.
Take a deep breath. The voice speaks
as if from another head. It's my voice.
A version of my voice.
A version of my ouma's voice.

And now, it says,
what would you put on the walls,
if you could choose anything? Imagine it.

I think about the Björk poster I used to have above my bed.
I think about a picture I once had of my sister and me,
dressed in tulle petticoats, beads strung around our necks.
In the picture, I am laughing, leaning forwards,
but Mora is staring ahead blankly, her mouth tense.

We are both so small.

I don't want anything on the walls.
I want them blank. I want to start over.
I want to burn my whole life down

and start again.

Try again, says the calm, steady voice. You can keep trying.

I imagine the walls covered in wallpaper.
Something intricate and colorful, a forest full of animals and flowers.
Walls and walls of yellow.

Antidote: *Hey, are you okay? Someone said you passed out at school*

I'm okay. Who told you that?

A few people saw you . . .

I forgot you're friends with everyone.

Haha, yeah

Antidote: *This weekend—how about we go to the beach?*

Which beach?

Boulders?

okay

Mamma complains the whole way
when she drops me off at Boulders Beach
on Saturday afternoon.

There's traffic on the road
that curves along the shoreline,
parked cars on either side
narrowing both lanes.

"Just get out here," she tells me. Drives off without waving.

I find the boy on the beach, jeans rolled up at his ankles.
He's standing between two egg-shaped boulders,
bare feet in the wash of the sea, slip-slops in his hand.
He's standing with his back to me. Looking out at the ocean.
The boulders cast their shadows, but he is bright beneath them.
And I want to hug him, but instead I tap him on the shoulder.

He turns around.
"Hey," I say. "What are you looking at?"
We stand side by side.
"Nothing. Just the world. You know."

Boulders Beach is small,
crowded with enormous rocks,
rocks Mora and I
used to pretend were giants.
We used to pretend they were asleep.
That they might wake up and eat us.
We raced across their faces.
In our games, I was always the one devoured first.

Now the boy and I walk on the sand,

passing the rocks, the penguins' cathedrals,

letting the cold water lap at our ankles.

"I thought maybe you'd be with your friends," I tell him.

"Which friends?"

"Your, um, millions of friends."

From far away, I can hear myself laughing. I'm really laughing.

"Hah. No. You're the only person I want to see these days."

"That's not true," I say.

"Okay, not really. But. It kind of is."

I stop, look into his eyes. "So you're saying I'm your favorite.

Out of all your friends."

"You're my favorite, yes. But I don't think we're just friends."

"We're not?" I can see he's trying to guess if I'm joking.

He laughs instead of answering. Then, quietly, I say,

"I know we're not just friends."

Moments later, we're in a cloud of pink-gold butterflies.

He takes my hand as I'm watching them.

I blush, looking down at the wet sand,

seawater sucking back, leaving a lacework of bubbles.

The boy doesn't look down. He's looking at the butterflies.

He doesn't ask me what they are.

He doesn't say he's heard my family is weird.

He watches them,

then puts out a hand and lets one

sit in his palm.

My face is as pink as the butterflies.
He touches my cheek.
Kisses me in a cloud of my own magic.
And it's a different kind of kiss.
Not the kind that chases every feeling away with its hunger.
The kind that feels as soft and safe as the inside of a rose.
I am transparent, right in front of him, the world going through me,
the ocean shushing itself, wind whistling through my ribs.

We keep walking,
and he's still holding my hand.

"How's your sister?" he asks. "Everyone at school,
they're always talking about her. She's in a clinic,
or something? Is she okay?" The word *sister*, that's what it is,
it's the word *sister* that reminds me why I need the hungry kind of kiss.
The pink-golden butterflies fly away from us, pushed ahead by a lashing wind.
I watch them go. "She's fine," I tell him.
Then I pause. "Actually, she's not fine.
She cuts herself really badly. That's why she's there."
"That sounds terrifying," he says.
"Honestly, it's become normal now. I know it sounds bad.
Obviously I love her—but it's also complicated."

I stop walking, concentrate. No wasps. Not now. Please.
Any time Mora's name is in my mouth, I have reason to worry.

"I don't want to talk about it."
"You say that a lot."
"I know."

We walk for a while in silence.

"Nell. I don't know if I've told you this. But I really like you."

I can hardly hear him.
Mora's in my head now, her voice loud, mocking:
"I really like you!" Her laugh. I start to cough.
Lean over, bracing against a boulder,
but the coughing won't stop.

"Are you okay?" the boy says, but I can't answer.
I try to face away from him. Because I know what's coming.
I try to hide it. But when I spit it out, he sees it:

the wasp in my hand.

PART FOUR

FIFTY-EIGHT DAYS AFTER THE WASPS

I haven't replied to any of the boy's messages.

At school, I can't even look at him. Every time I look at him,
I see the wasp, slick with saliva, sitting in my hand.

See myself dropping down to my haunches,
dunking my hands in the fizzing water. See the water carrying the wasp away.

I hear myself saying, "I have to go home,"
see myself messaging Mamma. I hear him say,
"Wait, Nell. Are you okay?"

I couldn't answer him.

I left him there, standing on the beach.

When he tried to follow me, I told him I wanted to be alone.

He's been so nice to me. That's the worst part.
Every message is just him asking how I am. Asking if I'm okay.

At school, he tries to take my hand,
and I pull away from him.
I can see it hurts, me pulling away, but he doesn't give up.

It makes the sticky black beetles come
and when I see them, I squirm inside
because I'm disgusting—I am actually disgusting.
The wasp I coughed out on the beach
was just one of thousands, one of swarms.

The way he looks at me—it's like
he thinks all of that doesn't matter.
It's like he doesn't even notice.
But when he does notice, when he finally sees it,
when he sees who I really am—

Late at night,
when I lie in bed,
staring at the ceiling,
and I think about the wasp
sitting in my hand,
twitching and loose,
filmy with mucus,
my bed fills with cockroaches
as big and hairy as kiwis,
white as maggots,
translucent as glue.
When they fly,
their hard shells split
and their wings
sound like electric razors.

I try not to watch them.
Try not to hear them.
But I have to watch them.
I have to hear them.

I'm filled with disgust.
For them. And for me.

Hey—just checking to see if you're okay?
You looked really sad at school . . .
I wish you'd talk to me

Hey Nell, just your resident checker-inner over here, um, checking in.
How was your day?

I saw this today and thought of you

Listened to this amazing song today and of course I thought of you!

Hey, just up late thinking of you

I know you said you didn't want to talk about it
But if you ever want to talk about it

I'm sorry if I weirded you out, sending you all these messages
If you just want to be friends . . . I would like that

"You can do better than this, Nell. It's up to you."

"You used to be one of my best students."

"You used to be so good."

When Mr. _____ talks, his words go right through me.

And when I leave his house,

down the steps,

three,

I don't think about him for another week,

a whole week,

and I don't touch the piano.

I don't think about him.

Until I am back.

Framed by the door.

A girl wearing a school dress,

a pair of jeans,

shorts and sandals.

Until he says,

"Come here. What are you standing over there for?"

There are nights when the insects come.
And it's not only one kind. One feeling.

There are nights when

the wasps, the glue-white roaches, the sticky beetles,
they arrive together, arrive like damp and kicked-up sand.

All at once, crawling across the floor,
sweeping around me like their own gust of wind.

I can't close my eyes.
I can't look away from them.

And the feelings are a rip current.

It's bad enough if it's just one thing—just one feeling—
but when it's all of them, their outlines blurring, their colors mixing,
their sounds raucous. I feel like the magic is going to end me.

There is no box you can put this in;
no neat container. All the parts of me I try to hide.

They come out roaring. Come out startling.
Churn slow across my vision.
They come out, true and ugly and bare.

That is the worst kind of night.

I'm on the threshold,
clutching sheet music to my chest.

I have a heat rash
dotted across my ribs and up my back
like a warped pink constellation,
welts unevenly spaced,
raised like arcane markings.

"Why're you standing in the doorway? Come in."

Mr. _____'s back is to me. His head is bent.
Doing something at his desk.
Writing words and erasing them.
Dusting fragments away with his hand.

His hand.

Hand around my waist.

He turns to me, swiveling in his chair,
and I'm stepping back, scratching my ribs.

"Did something bite you?" he says.
"No, it's just a heat rash."
"That doesn't look like a heat rash."

Quiet.

His wet mouth.

"Can I see?"

I don't say anything.

He's closer now,
the chair on wheels scooted
closer, closer.

His fingers are on the hem of my shirt,
and he folds the fabric up.

Freeze.
Fingers cold on my ribs.

He lifts the fabric more.

"Looks bad," he says.
He's peering up my shirt now.

Looking at my skin.
At my ribs.
My skin like fleshy bubble wrap.

He's looking up my shirt.

I push the hem down, move away, move back.
Back against the piano behind me.

He frowns for a second. Then laughs. Shakes his head.
"What's gotten into you?"

At my next lesson with Mr. _____,
my fingers only hit wrong notes
for thirty minutes straight.

At least I've given him something to worry about
so he doesn't have time to ask
if my heat rash has healed.

"You'd better pull up your socks," he says.

Like he's a nice guy.
Like he hasn't looked up my shirt.

It's desperation. In the end. That makes me reply to the boy.

It's the wasps and the roaches and the beetles,
coming, coming back, over and over.

Hey . . .
Sorry I haven't been replying to your messages
And sorry for being so weird
Just going through a bit of a hard time right now

In a few minutes, my phone pings with his response:
Come to my place tomorrow after school?

I think about it. About the glue-white roaches. And the wasps.
About what I will have to risk. And what I will gain.

Sure. You mean like come home with you?

Yeah, if that's easier

Mamma doesn't mind me going to a boy's house.
She's just glad she doesn't have to fetch me from school.
She's sitting on the sofa with her knees up,
eating condensed milk darkened with cocoa powder.

She's as young as I am,
her eyes bright and wet.

"Come watch with me," she says.

I sit next to her, my head on her shoulder.

"I love you, baby," she says.

"I love you, too, Mamma."

It's just the two of us.
At the boy's house.
After Cole drops us off.

The boy unlocks the front door
and we fall inside,
dropping our bags, pulling off our blazers.
He closes the door behind me and kisses me,
hands in my hair, lips on my neck.

"I missed you," he tells me.
"Are your parents out?"
"At work." Leads me to the kitchen,
offers to make me anything I want.
"I don't want anything," I say.
"Nothing? You sure?"

I'm trying not
to think about
the wasp I coughed
into my hand
on the beach
but the image keeps
showing up,
dark at the edges.

"Just you," I say, kissing him.
"Let's go to your room. I want to go to your room."

What happens in the boy's room is I forget that wasps have ever existed.

When his skin touches my skin, the room fills with giant black butterflies,
butterflies the size of two open hands,
butterflies the color of evening, twilight, midnight.
He's looking into my eyes so intently he doesn't notice them at first.
"Uh—whoa," he says, lying next to me. It's strange,
watching your own desire, your own sharpest wanting,
drifting up to the ceiling. The boy kisses me again,
and I'm unbuttoning my dress and his hands are under it, searching.
When his hands are on my skin. I remember why I have it.
I remember that I am alive. I remember that everything outside me—
moons, whole skies of stars—is sheltered in me, too.
That we each walk around, a world contained.
Waiting for someone to remind us.

Later,

the boy gives me one of his hoodies to wear,
makes me a cup of tea.

We sit on the sofa,
watching a cooking show with the sound down,
his leg pressed against my leg, his arm around me.

I fall asleep and
when I wake up, the entire house is filled
with pink-and-gold butterflies. It's hours like that,
hours of happy quiet,

until Cole comes home.

"Mom and Dad are still busy at the restaurant," he tells the boy.
"I'm gonna have some friends over."

"Do you want to stay?" the boy says to me.

"Okay," I tell him.

Cole's friends

put on music
and talk loudly over it,
talk loudly
over each other,
talk like
they're competing
for most words per minute.

They drink beer.
They ignore us.

I'm relieved the butterflies
are gone.

I don't want
anyone
besides the boy
to see them.

When I go to the kitchen
to get a glass of water,
Cole, Khaya, and some other guy
are arguing about whether a band
can be considered good
if it has a female vocalist.

"With the exception of Garbage—maybe," says Khaya, "a girl's voice,
I don't know, doesn't have the same edge."
"You sing, right?" says Cole,
clamping his arm around my waist.
"What do you think?"
I start to move away, but Khaya says:
"Seriously, though, name one female vocalist that—"
"Björk," I say. "Susanne Sundfør. Agnes Obel—"
"Wait. Do you exclusively listen to Scandi pianists?" Cole is laughing.
"Sharon Van Etten," I say. "Angel Olsen. Julien Baker—"
". . . the point is," the other boy is saying,
"a girl's voice, the softness. Doesn't match."
I swallow. "What about Beth Gibbons? Portishead?
The fact that her voice is soft makes the band good. It's the contrast—"
"No—what makes the band good is the musicians," says Khaya.
"They're the ones who write all the music."
I decide to ignore the fact
that he's just implied
that singers aren't musicians.
"Beth Gibbons writes the vocal parts," I say.
"The lyrics, the melodies. The songs wouldn't be
what they are without—"
"But imagine those songs in a guy's voice," says Khaya, his eyes wide.

I realize this is the universe they want:

a universe in which
every voice
is a guy's voice.

That's when I walk away.

I find the boy outside, sitting in the dark garden.

"Hey," I say.
"Hey."
"Sorry. I got cornered."
"Cole?"
"Yeah."
The boy looks at me, but I'm not sure what the look means.
Then he says, "Today was—"
"I loved today." I have to glance away when I tell him.
He puts his arm around me,
dips his shoulder so I can rest my head.

A little later
I go to the bathroom,
pushing past boys
who won't
move out of the way.
Who look at me too closely.
Who don't see me at all.

When I come out,
Cole is standing
in the passage,
laughing with his friends.
I can tell
he's had a lot to drink.
I don't know
how the boy
lives like this.
Cole. He takes up
too much space.
He makes the house
feel cramped.

"Nell!" he says.
"Hey! Nell! Come tell us some more
about the Scandinavian music scene!"

A handful of wasps appears
in front of my face,
darkening my vision.

I watch them,
electrified with anger,
a jolt of ice and heat.

Tear my eyes away from them,
keep walking. I don't want the wasps to come.
Not here. Not now. Not more of them.
Not in front of him.

Cole lumbers over to me,
puts a hand against the wall
over my head. Leans in.
Kisses   me.

He's kissing me.
And I am kissing him   back.

Instead of wasps, the hunger,
the sparkling pull
of velvet butterflies.

One of them, two of them,
brushing my flushed cheeks.

Instead of the wasps.
Anything instead of the wasps.

I can hear Cole's friends clapping,
making sounds of approval.

Cole takes his lips off mine
and steps back. Bats the butterflies away, annoyed.
"I knew you'd rather kiss me than him."

He looks over his shoulder at his brother.

At the boy.

Who is standing
there, looking at me.

Outside,
on the front steps,
trying
to figure out
what just
happened.

What I just did.

I didn't want the wasps to come.
That was the thing.
And when the black-velvet butterflies are there,
they chase the wasps away.

Like desire is the one feeling
that pushes all the others to the background.

It was the wasps,
but it was also—

it was also that the boy is too nice to me.

Something about Cole was so familiar.
The way he mocked me, loomed over me.
The way he took what he wanted.

Something about it felt safer.

The boy is behind me now,
slipping out the door, saying my name.

"Nell."

I can't turn around.

"Did he—force you?"

"No."

I hear him breathe out. "Then—"

"I wanted to kiss him."

This isn't a lie,
and the thought
makes a handful of sticky black beetles
appear on the brick step, writhing.
I stare at them,
the shame thick inside me.

"But—okay. I guess I thought we were . . ."

We are. But.

I turn around. "You should be with someone who's nicer than me."

I've been using him. Of course I have.
His name is still saved under *antidote* in my phone.

"You are nice to me," he says.
"I only kissed you because I was panicking. That day. At school.
You were just the first boy who looked at me. So."
"Why were you panicking?"
"I told you—things are . . ."

Mamma's car appears, trawling through the dark,
and I run down the steps, fast, before I can finish my sentence.

Climb in the car and wave. Like everything's normal.

When I wake up the next morning,
my room is full of wasps, moving like liquid.

They are smoke. They are atmosphere.

I stare at them, can't look away,
can't stop the anger
from pushing its hands
into me.

Someone is banging on my door.

I guess I've gotten into the habit of locking it.

I look around at the blank walls, blinking,
peering through the wing-storm.

Hear my name. Mamma's voice.

"Nell? Are you okay? Nell. Open this door."

Open the door. Open the door.
But I can't open the door.

"Nell?" Rattling the handle.

I drag myself to standing.

"Mamma. I'm fine," I yell.

Anger in my blood. Anger in my voice.

"Open the door."

"I can't."

The wasps are loud. They're swarming me,
throwing their bodies against me.

I can't look away. And the heat inside me. It's getting worse and worse.

"Are they hurting you?" I hear her say.

Not exactly.

"No," I say.

"Then they won't hurt me."

"Mamma—"

"Nell. Open. This. Door."

Mamma is thirty-eight today.

She's standing in my bedroom.

Surrounded by wasps.

More and more

and more and more

and more and more of them.

She amplifies them. Amplifies me.

And I'm so angry with her, with Dad, Ouma, all of them.

Mora. Cole and Mr. _____. I am angry at myself.

I look at Mamma, in the black swirl. Look at the wasps.

I am swallowed up by them. They are never-ending.

Mamma is watching me. Her face is still and pale.

I don't want her to see it. See all of it. Like this.

But she won't close her eyes. She won't leave the room.

I can feel the heat rising in my body. I want to scream.

She stands there, watching them whip the room into shadow.

Reaches for me, but I pull away. "Leave me alone," I tell her.

She grabs my elbow, starts to drag me out the room.

I think she's trying to get me away from them, to stop it,

and I struggle, but she speaks close to my ear:

"You need space," she says. "Space for them to get big."

There are wasps in the air around us.
Wasps against the clouds.

There are wasps sitting on every branch,
on the flaking bark of the bottlebrush trees,
in the glossed leaves of the Australian brush cherry,
blackening the insides of all my mother's roses.

They hover over the surface of the pool.
They cling to the windows.

I squint at them, mouth closed, biting my lip.
Mamma puts her arm around me. Tightly.

"You can be angry," she says. "You can be angry."

I watch them multiply, watch them churn like a storm.

"Let them get big," she says. "As big as you need them to get."

The wasps are black-hole huge, they're a mouth,
they're eating the sun and the garden.

I think about the boy.
What he would say if he saw this.
If he saw the disasters that can come out of me.
Then I remember: he already kind of has.
He already knows.

How I can blast
something
apart.

It turns out that I haven't died.

Mamma hasn't either,
even if she has gotten a little older:
thirty-nine, forty, forty-one, forty-two.

The wet garden is covered in wasps.
Their fat, hot bodies sitting on everything,
legs twitching. The ugliness,
the net of them,
flung over the world.

But I haven't died.

I haven't died when they are taking the sky over, haven't died
when they start to slow, when they start to drop
out of the air, onto the ground. When they lie, dead, in the pool.

At some point, I notice Mamma has taken my hand.

She's shaking her head.

"What?" I bark,
the energy still in me, pushing words
I wouldn't normally say
out of my mouth. But she can take it.

"Just promise me," she says. Not looking at me.
"Just promise. You won't ever hide again."

I hid. And I was invisible.
I was invisible. So I hid.
I hid. So I was invisible.
I was invisible. And I hid.

We sweep up the dead wasps
with a rake and a garden broom.

The rake and broom Dad uses
for dried leaves on Sundays.

Mamma helps me.

She sweeps the path, the brick patio.
I rake the lawn.
I fish them out of the pool.

We bury the wasps in the flower beds.
We let the loam take them.
The wind is still, like it's waiting.

And it's good to know there's something solid under me.
Earth as old as history.
Something solid that can take it.
Take whatever happens.

Break it down
and turn it into
something
with bright petals.

I've been staring at my phone for days.
Waiting for the boy to message me.

I guess I finally convinced him.
That he doesn't want to know me.

I change the boy's name in my phone.

From *antidote* to *Shay*.

Dad fetches Mora from the clinic. Brings her home.

She stands at the top of the path, wearing a woolly hat. She's shivering.

"Welcome home, Mori," Mamma says,

walks to her, hugs her. Mora shakes harder.

Mamma walks her down the path while Dad watches.

Later, I find Mora in her room. Looking around. Looking at the walls.

Like she's in someone else's house. Like she doesn't know how she got here.

For days,
Mamma and I
are best friends,
because she's young
but not too young,
because she shares
music with me,
because she's a little
happier than usual,
because she laughs
in the car
at my jokes.

But after a while,
I can feel
her start to
slowly turn away.
I feel her
shoulder turning,
turning towards a window,
towards the world
moving alongside the car,
the world streaming
behind her steering wheel.

When I try to reach her,
when I try to say,
"Come back,"
she snaps at me.
"You're being clingy, Nell."

And I know
the only thing
that I can do
is wait.

When she turns
back towards me,
she will forget
she ever turned away.

But I won't.
I will remember.

One night,
after Mora's been home
for a few weeks,
she goes walking.
Doesn't come back
until morning.

Mamma takes one look at her in the kitchen and goes to bed.

So it's just me and Mora,
waiting for the kettle to boil,
trying not to see each other.

"Did you get your magic?" she says, like she's only just realized
it was my birthday a few months ago.

"Yeah. Yeah, I did."

"And?" One of her eyebrows flattens.

"And?"

"I bet yours is perfect. I bet it's, like, shitting cupcakes or something."

I rub my eyes. A wasp appears. Mora doesn't notice it.

"You don't want to tell me? Oh my God, am I right?" She laughs.

"Mora. You're being mean."

Her new laugh stutters at the end. "Tell me what your magic is. Please."

But her begging voice doesn't work on me anymore.

See the wasp
out the corner of my eye.

The kettle starts to whistle.

When Mora and I
were little,
Dad would take us
to Llandudno Beach
on Saturday mornings.

To give Mamma
a break, some peace and quiet,
the house to herself.

The sand as white as heaven.
The waves, violent as fire.

Even in summer,
the sea was freezing.

We'd run in
like we were fighting
some kind of war.

As soon as the water came up to our ribs,
the cold would knock our voices out of us, and we'd stand there,
teeth chattering, clinging to each other.

It was always a competition. Who would run back to the shore first.

The water ached through us like a signal.
I could never take it for long. Mora always outlasted me.

Even then,
she used to stare me down.

Mora doesn't want
to go back to *that school*
(the words are loud,
filling the kitchen, accompanied by
the slamming of the fridge).
I think about the graffiti in the bathroom.
I think about Mina Tredoux saying,
"Your sister is a freak."
I think about Saskia, how clean she is now,
how she scrubbed herself of ever knowing us.
And I think about all the teachers
who think it's a compliment to tell me
that I am nothing like my sister.
I hate them—Mina Tredoux, and Saskia, and the teachers—
but I also hate how Mora is screaming
at Mamma in the kitchen.

Mora changes schools.

For a while, Mamma is in her thirties.
And she still dresses like she's twenty-two
but she drives us to school and never goes
over the speed limit.

First Mora gets dropped off. Then me.

We listen to music in the car. Turned up loud.

Mora sways in the front seat, dancing,
which makes Mamma smile in a scared sort of way.

After Mamma drops Mora off,
she talks to me about her.
All the way to school.

Mora won't go to a therapist.
If Mamma makes her go,
Mora plays games with them,
tries to shock them, tells them stories.
Mora told Mamma that when people
stare at her arms she thinks it's because
the cuts just aren't deep enough.
Mora comes home from school
with pages and pages of drawings instead of notes.

Mostly I try to say soothing things.
But sometimes the car fills with wasps,
a panicked march of ants coating the windows.
Sometimes the thick-gray moths
come out of my mouth instead of words.

When that happens,
Mamma pulls the car over
and waits until they die.
Waits. Then says:
"Let's just have some quiet."

I practice the wasps
like I'm practicing
a musical instrument.

Practice
watching them swarm and swirl.
Practice
letting the anger into me.

So it doesn't have to force its way
through me
like the wind sucked
down a narrow street
in town.

In my room. In the garden. I watch them.
Flying through the air.

Most days,
I still hate to look at them.

But I'm learning
to see.

To see them
as messengers.

They do not make me feel good.
They are not gentle or kind.

But they remind me of the truth.

Mamma looks at me differently.
And so does Dad.

I regret this.

But I   am also   relieved.

The strangest part is Mora.

Mora, watching the wasps with me.

"You're stronger than I thought you were," she says one morning.

She's sitting on top of the wooden table under the bottlebrush trees.

Chin tilted, cigarette smoke coming out of her mouth.

What I know is I've always been strong.

Just haven't spent enough time showing it.

The wasps have given me my anger.

I can feel it now. So I say,

"Why are you so mean to me, Mora?"

The music under her skin is raucous.

I can't hear it,

because she's not bleeding,

but I can feel it,

filling the air between us.

Energy with nowhere to go.

She looks away and frowns. "You have everything," she says.

I let the words drag through the air, slow as aeroplanes.

"I don't have everything."

"You have everything I want."

I want to ask her
what it is that she wants.
And why we can't both have something
at the same time.

But when I tear my eyes from the wasps
to look back at the table, she's gone.

At school. Close my eyes. Grit my teeth. Push past the elbows.

I walk right into the boy. Look up at his face and

three huge black beetles, sticky as syrup,
crawl up the back of my neck.

I grab at them, pull them off me, throw them onto the floor.

I don't even care if anyone sees them.
I just don't want them on me.

But my eyes are drawn to their shiny backs,
to the dark trail
they leave behind.

The shame winces into me.

Elbows all around. Moving, close-clung forest. Shut my eyes again.

"Nell. Can we talk?"
"I don't want to talk," I say, already walking away. Push past.

He follows me.

"I really liked you." He says this close to my ear,
his lips almost touching the spot where,
seconds ago, three fat beetles
sat on my skin like blood blisters.

There are more of them now, on the floor,
crushed under other people's feet. Crawling towards me.
I hear someone say, "Ew—oh my God."
I watch them crawl. The shame curdles.

"I really *like* you," the boy says.
"But it's—I'm on one side of a door.
And you're on the other." This makes me stop.

"Sometimes," he says, "when we were in your room.
You were there. But you were so far away.
At the same time."

I keep walking. But he keeps catching up.

"Do you know what I mean?" he says.
"I don't even care that you kissed my brother.
Or if he kissed you, or whatever.
I don't care if you want to be friends,
or if you don't. I just wanted to tell you.
That I always liked you.
That I still—like you."

He stops, but I keep walking.
This time, he doesn't follow.

There are sticky black beetles
on the dead flower path
right up to Mr. _____'s front door.

I squash them under my feet.

There's a sticky black beetle
on one of the clean windows.

On the back of my hand.

Stare at them.
Feel it.

I slip inside,
walk down the carpeted passage
to the narrow study.

He's sitting at his desk, back to me, head bowed, writing something.

"Nell," he says. "Come in."

I've missed a few lessons
since he looked up my shirt
and he's pissed off about it,
like I'm the one who's let him down.

His voice is flat. His voice is out of tune.

"Sit at the piano. We'll start with scales." I freeze in the doorway.

This is different. Something's different.

"Go on," he says, turning around in his chair when I don't move.
"We've got a lot to get through."

I sit at the piano. Start to play the scales.
I haven't been practicing at all, though, and my hands are clumsy.

He stands behind me, hands on my shoulders, holding me down.
"You know I only do this because you want me to."

Fingertips smoothing the hair at the nape of my neck,
just under my ponytail. "You want me to. Don't you?"

My hands stop moving over the keys.

A black beetle crawls along my collarbone.

I don't reach for it.
I don't move it.
I let it sit there.

Mr. _____ jumps. "What's . . ."

And there are more of them.

Across my chest,
on my shoulders,
up my back.

Shiny as a breastplate.

They're on the carpet.
They're on the pedals of the piano.

Mr. ____ has stepped back.
His hands are deep in his pockets.
He's watching the beetles.
Watching me watch them.
He's backing away.

"Disgusting," he says, and shakes his head, mouth open.
"What is wrong with you?"

The wasps come
without warning,
filling the room.

I stare at them.
Let the anger enter.

And. For the first time.
I am glad. They are here.

The wasps are an army.

Churning and diving. Flowing like poured liquid.

Inside me: darkness and fire.
Light that speaks of the shadows.

Mr. ____ puts his arms up to cover his face.
He backs into the shelf of books.

Then he's crouching on the ground,
hands over his head. Trembling.

A short, pale man,
a little chubby.
Thinning hair.
He flaps his hands
to get the wasps away.

They don't hurt him. They don't sting anyone.
They're not that kind of wasp.
But they scare him. And they still him.
And they crouch him in the corner.

They give me
the words
I have to say.

"I'm never coming back."

Outside, I stand on the curb.

See his wife's face in the window.

A ghost behind warped glass.

Take my phone out, message Mamma.

Mamma fetches me,

but when I tell her I don't want to go back
she doesn't like the idea.

"You'll regret it," she says.
"I know it's challenging.
But you should keep going with it."

"I won't regret it."

"Nell."

"Mamma."

The car drones towards our house.

The silence. It's a stone in my mouth.

I have to learn
to talk around it.

"He's—he's been touching me.
He looked up my shirt."

Mamma snaps her head to the left.
"Who?" She takes a corner, fast.

"Mr. ____."

"What?"

She's upset now, scanning the road
like she's looking for something.
Her age changes and she's seventeen.

"What?" she says again.

"I'm not going back," I tell her. "I won't regret it."

At night, Mora comes to my bedroom,
knocks softly on the half-open door.

"Hey."
"Hey."
"Mamma said . . ."
"Yeah."
"He really– touched you?"

ı look away. I'm sitting on my bed, notebook open,
the heavy pen in my hand. But I can't write anything.

After all the noise.
All the humming and buzzing.
All I have is silence.

"How long?"
"I don't know."
"Why didn't you tell anyone?"

How can I tell her
that her name
is so loud
it fills the house.
How can I tell her
that her music
drowns out everything.

How can I tell her
that I didn't know
if it was my fault.

How can I tell her.
This kind of thing.
It doesn't happen.
To the good sister.

I sit at the piano. Rest my fingers on the keys.

Come on, Nell. Play a chord. The sound shivers into me.
I play a simple progression, nothing fancy, nothing complicated.

Everything is complicated.
I want the music to be simple.

Start to sing over the chords, wordlessly finding my way,
my voice getting louder and louder.

Then I see the stick insects.

Blue stick insects. Pens bursting with night-dark ink.

I watch them
track across the keys
until the tears
drip off my chin.

The berg wind comes down, hot air blustering from a height,
whipping down the mountain like the memory of fire,
drying my curls when I get out the shower, wicking the oil off my skin.
It comes like a messenger, bearing leaves and loose twigs.

I stand outside, hands open, thinking about how the whole world
bent to Mora's will, bent to the shape of Mamma's sadness,
bent to Mr. _____'s wanting. But there are some things
that Mora and Mamma and Mr. _____ can't hold in their hands.

Some things they could never own.

My wasps.
The light I see.
My body. Me.

The berg wind blows and blows for days without end,
hush and whisper, saying its sayings,
saying things I have only ever understood
with the soles of my feet.

When it finally dies down, the rain comes after it,
soothing the ground, gentle, interminable.
Gray rain. Rain like tears. Rain like sighing.

It drips off the eaves,
washing clear every window.

Every clear window
looks out onto the garden
where the sticks and twigs
the wind brought down
lie soaked, waiting to be raked away,
waiting to be threaded
into nests by birds,
waiting to mulch into soil,
into dirt that will grow a new thing.
It's this mess that makes me feel ready.
The way the soft rain
touched every spent thing.
The way it fell on everything,
kissed everything, like everything
belonged to its falling,
like everything, living and dead,
deserved not to drown
but to drink.

I message Shay.

Hey. I know you probably don't want to talk to me

But. Could we talk?

Because I want to tell you

everything

I meet Shay in Newlands Forest,
walking past Ouma's house,
the same way I walked on the day
the wasps first came.

And now we—
me, and Shay—
walk under
the tall pine trees.

Forest floor
coated with moss,
thick as fur coats,
and lichen like crochet,
the sound of water
slowly shaping rock.

I sit down on a fallen trunk, the roots like torn ligaments.
He sits, too. His hand on the damp bark between us.

"I wanted to tell you—"
"Everything."
"Yeah."

Here's the thing. Talking about this stuff.
You never know the difference
between the beginning and the end.
Everything's tangled. The same bloody knot.

But I start with Mora.
Because everything starts with Mora.

And then I tell him about Mamma.
I tell him about the magic.
The butterflies. Beetles. Wasps.

I tell him about Mr. _____.

He listens, looking down.

I tell him why I kissed him that first day.

Tell him that now I want to kiss him
for other reasons.

Tell him why I kissed Cole.
Tell him I'm sorry.

I tell him if he never wants to speak to me again
after this, I'll understand.

When I'm done, there's silence between us,
ringing like the wire of a just-played piano.

"I always knew the butterflies were you," says Shay.
"That praying mantis in the car. And the wasp on the beach.
I know it doesn't make any sense. But it made sense to me.
When I saw them. Because they were just—you.
Like the color of your hair. The way you talk."

It feels like the trees are leaning in.

"I can see you, Nell. I've always been able to see you."

It's hard, but I look into his eyes.
Let him see me.
Peer into the seeing.

It's a burn, being seen like that.
It's unbearable, like putting your
freezing feet in a hot bath.

"I'm sorry I'm such a mess," I say.

Between us,
along the fallen trunk,
there are slow-crawling stick insects,
needle-delicate,
blue as evening mountains.

I watch them. Can't help but watch them.

Shay comes closer, kisses me. He tastes my tears; I taste his.

"We're all messes," he says.
"And you don't have to say sorry anymore.
I'm sorry for letting my brother treat you like that.
For not standing up to him.
I've never really stood up to him."

"I know all about that," I say, a laugh hurting my throat.

"I know you do."

Afterwards,

we walk through the forest, light dancing through the still branches,

filtered, softer when it lands at our feet
on the moss and the moldering leaves.

Mist falls between the trees like curtains lowering.

The whole world is just light, playing with our eyes.
That's what Mamma says.

But there's also light in us. Light that comes from us. Light between us.

That's the light
I'm living in now.

I write Shay a message when I get home:

Hey . . .

Here's one of my songs, in case you want to hear it . . .

I attach the bad, crackly voice note.

. . .

. . .

. . .

Whoa, that's beautiful. So cool that you can just do that!

I listen to the voice note
over and over,
just to remind myself
what I sound like,
just to hear it again.
The whoa,
and the beautiful.

I have stuck
my Björk poster
on the wall
again.

When I sit at the piano,
she stares at me,
into me,

like she knows everything I know,
like she knows something I don't.

I'm trying to write a song
but the chorus keeps looping back on itself,
won't go anywhere.

The melody meets a wall.
Stops.

I lift my fingers off the piano's keys,
turn on the stool,
flop onto my bed, sigh it out.

Little flies buzz against my window
and my chest fizzles until they die.

Close my eyes,
hum the chorus to myself,
let it go anywhere,
let it linger and rush.

Then the song finds its way
like a bird
that's been trapped
in your kitchen
for hours
finally finding
the open window.

My room
is full of ladybugs.

The bright feeling they bring
clouds into me,
intense as incense.

I watch them.
Circling like yellow suns.

They float, unhurried as sunrise,
and when they die, they fall slowly to the floor.

For hours afterwards,
my room is warm.
Like it remembers magic.

Like it's saying to me:

"Do you see
how everything—
everything—
can change?"

You never think it's going to happen.

Until it happens.

Egyptian geese flying over the field,
the sky behind them clear of clouds,
pale blue and gold at the same time,
and the green of the grass, especially green,
sits in the clear palm of the morning.

A light in me like my bones are floating,
like the sky pulling upwards, tied to strings around my wrists.

You never think it's going to happen.

Until it happens.

The oak trees with their patterned bark.
The ground under my feet.

Around me. A shimmer of color like a sigh.

Dragonflies.

I send Sabine a video. Of the dragonflies.

She replies with the heart-eyes emoji.

Are they joy?

More like hope, I type.
Like the feeling of spring coming back after a long, wet winter.
Morning after a bad night.

Got it, she says. More heart eyes, and eyes as stars, and a few rainbows.

I type the next words quickly. *I get wasps, too. When I'm angry.*

Good, says Sabine. *Every girl needs her anger.*

Every girl.

Needs her anger.

Mora's music again.

Seeping up the passage like water under the door.
It wakes me. Middle of the night. I shove my way into her room.

She's kneeling on the floor. With a razor blade in her hand.
Trailing it across the top of her forearm. Pressing it down.

Blue stick insects, thick as arteries and the darkest possible blue,
blue before it becomes black. My heart: a perfect circle of indigo.

Then ants, their bodies fat, legs long and crooked.
They move against my arms, living sleeves.

It all takes one second, two,
and then the wasps
rip through the room like wind.

It's the wasps that make Mora turn her face to me.

It's the wasps that make me say,
"Mora, what are you doing?"

"Get out," she says. Then screams the words: "Get out!"

The music beats against the walls.

More wasps. They explode out of the windows, into the garden.

I think about how
we buried the dead wasps
in the earth.
How the earth could take them.

How I can take this.

I walk to her, hold her wrist,
take the razor blade from her pinched fingers.

She screams at me again. And I don't scream back. But I don't back down.

PART FIVE

EIGHTY-NINE DAYS AFTER THE WASPS

Mora is back at the clinic
and it's time to visit her again

so Mamma stands at the door, waiting.
Handbag on her shoulder. She's thirty-three today.

She's watching Dad crossing the lawn,
walking in diagonals.
He's talking and talking on his phone.

"Ready?" she says, sensing me behind her.

"Yep," I say,

and we step out the door,
start walking up the path.

I call out to him. "Dad."

He doesn't hear me.

"Dad."

He looks up, raises his eyebrows.

"Come with us."

He points at his phone.

"Dad's busy," says Mamma.

I walk up to him,
right up to him,
put my hand in his hand.

"Come with us. Please. We need you there."

Mora doesn't ignore us.
I think she's shocked to see Dad.

"Hey," she says. Her voice is a crackle.

I can feel the music under her skin when I take her hand.

I wish Ouma were here, too.
Wish I could bring every person
who's ever been part of our family.
Hundred-year-old ghosts.
Everyone. No matter what they did.

All of us.
It'll take all of us.

Mamma's eyes are wet, and she's sixteen.

Dad stretches his arm across the space
between the two lines of chairs. To touch Mora's fingers.

Her face is gray, like someone has charcoaled her cheekbones.

"Mora," I say. "Mori."

Mora's lips part. She stares past me. For a second.
Then her eyes find me again.

"We just want you to be okay," says Mamma.
She moves over to sit next to Mora.

I move, too. Pressing against Mamma.
And Dad sits on Mora's other side.

And Mora cries.
She cries and she cries.

And Dad just strokes her hair,
saying, "Shhh."

Dad drops me off at Ouma's house.
She wants to see me. Tell me something.

"When I first got my magic.
I thought I would never get used to it.
All those rooms inside me,
always moving and changing,
the light on the floor
and the words all vibrating
against the walls.
I thought I would have to live in a box,
in a one-room shed, in a dark forest.
I thought I wouldn't survive it.
Even now, sometimes when I'm falling asleep,
I catch myself getting overwhelmed.
The sounds and the movements.
They build up in me.
My chest feels jumbled, loud,
like a drawer full of loose change.
But I just breathe."

"How did you deal with it?" I ask her.

"I've realized, Nell. The magic.
It's only another shade of purple.
Do you know what I mean?
It's an extra shade.
It can't hurt me. It adds to me.
Adds. Doesn't take away."

"Mora's is hurting her, though.
Her magic. It really is hurting her," I say.

"Is it?"

I imagine Ouma holding

all the rooms
in the house
in her hands.

"Mora is hurting herself, Nell.
And that's a terrible thing.
And we need to help her.
We need to get her the help she needs.
And we're working on that.
But did you ever think.
Maybe, even if she didn't have the magic.
Maybe she would do the same thing.
We don't know."

I sip my tea.

"Maybe—I imagine, I'm only imagining—
but maybe the music inside her,
if she's quiet enough,
maybe she will hear it.
Without having to hurt herself.
There must be other ways.
To hear what is inside us."

"Sometimes," I say, "I can sense it. Even when she's not—"

Ouma nods. "It's a part of her.
She doesn't have to hurt herself.
That is not the only way
she can live with the music.
Just like—well,
I didn't have to live in a shed,
alone, in a dark, dark place."

She looks out the window,
at the rain-wet ferns.
At the way autumn
makes everything greener.

"I struggle. To go to hotels," she says.
"To malls and things.
But, you know, when I'm in someone's house.
I know the house. I really know it.
It adds, Nell. And I really believe
it can be that way for Mora."

"But my magic.
Compared to hers.
It's nothing.
It feels so unfair."

What she has to carry.
What I don't have to carry.

I think of her words: *You have everything I want.*

"Do you think it's nothing?" says Ouma.
"I'm not sure about that.
Either way, we all get the magic we get.
We have to decide for ourselves.
What to do with it.
In another world, Mora's magic
might have been harmless, and yours
could have driven you to hurt yourself.
Are you hurting yourself?"

Am I
hurting
myself?

Maybe.
Sometimes.

"Maybe. Sometimes."

"Well."

Ouma's hugs are different
from Mamma's,
which always feel like semicolons,
like she can only bear them for so long.

Ouma holds me.
She lets me stay still.
Stay as long as I want.

So maybe it's complicated.
All this difficult magic.

Maybe it doesn't make any sense at all.
Maybe it makes our lives harder.

Maybe it's a part of everything.
Maybe it belongs.

Maybe it's another shade of purple.
Maybe it has made us
who we are supposed to be.

Maybe there is no supposed to be.
Only this. What is here. Now.

Maybe there are bad things about the magic,
and good things, too.

Maybe it doesn't mean anything,
and maybe it means everything,
everything in the world,
and maybe the truth of it changes
from moment to moment.

Maybe it's the most important thing about us.
Maybe it's the least important thing about us.

Maybe it is both. Maybe it is both.

Because the thing is.

I used to think that the wasps
were bad.

But now I know
better.

Now I know

that almost everything

is always both.

I used to think
that in order to live
a good life.

Be a good person.
A person who really tries.

I had to keep
the wasps away.

But now I know.
I have to take care of my anger.
Now I know.
It wants to take care of me.

"Ouma?"

"Yes, liefie?"

"Mamma told me. She said.
She said she should never have had children."

Ouma is calm.
"Perhaps I shouldn't have had children either."

A spray of yellow stink bugs fizzes on my shoulder,
noxious and neon. I let the shock travel right through me.

Ouma watches the bugs.

"But that doesn't matter, does it?
The fact is, I did have children,
and your mamma had children. Had you.
And the only thing that matters right now is.
Well, you have been given something.
Haven't you? You have been given a life."

I have been given a life.

I have. Been given. A life.

Shay:

Want to meet the band this Saturday?

(We're not very good. Not as good as Cole. Just warning you.)

Me:

I'm sure you're good

Shay:

Want to come?

Me:

Yes

Shay's band is three guys who wear shirts that are way too big for them.

They've got a drum set, an electric guitar, a bass, a few amps and pedals.
Knotted cables in the middle of the garage.

When they play, the music is physical. A force, wired and growling.
It rises up from the ground. It makes me smile uncontrollably.

"Our singer left," Shay says when the other two are rolling up the cables.
"If you want to. We're looking for someone. That's all I'm saying."

"I don't know."

"You didn't like it."

"I liked it. I don't know if I have that kind of thing—inside me.
You know. That kind of sound."

I remember the conversation Cole and his friends
were having in the kitchen on the night he kissed me—
the night I kissed him back—
about how girls can't sing in bands.

A wasp appears.
An indigo stick insect like a pin in my hair.
Dragonflies, gold as medallions.
I let it all go into me.

"I could try," I tell Shay. Shake my head like I don't believe it.

He calls the others back. I guess he's explaining.
They nod and plug everything in again.

They play those big, hungry chords. And I stand in front of the mic.

The next time we visit Mora, she's screaming again.
Not just at me. At everyone.

Dad holds her when she's like that, holds her still.

Sometimes it helps.

This time, after she stops screaming,

she says:

"I want to get better.
I really want to get better."

"That's good, Mori," Mamma says.
"See how it goes," says Dad.

And I just say, "Mora. When you're better. Do you want to swim?"

Afterwards,
we are silent in the car.

Dad stares straight ahead,
steering us through.

Mamma is sixteen.
Hold her hand the whole way home.

Dad goes for a run
when we get back

and Mamma starts making dinner,
pulling onions, green peppers, mincemeat
out of the fridge. Lighting the stove.

I leave her in the kitchen,

walk outside,
into the garden,
which belongs
to the evening
now.

I stand still,
and I wait.

Wait for wasps,
wait for gray moths,
wait for the blue
stick insects.
Wait for ladybugs
like yellow stars,
the iron and itch of ants,
the milk-slick of roaches.

I wait
for
whatever
wants
to come.

For the strange visitors
who know
the inside of me.

An hour later, Dad's still out,
running his way through the almost dark.

Mamma's left dinner on the table.
With a note: *love you, baby*

Take the plate to my room and that's when I see the dragonflies.
Catching the last of the day's light, bringing it to me like a gift.

These days, the dragonflies always come after the wasps.
            After the roaches and flies; after blue pinpricks my throat.

Their wings are like little mirrors, stealing light, carrying it away,
                    bringing it back and back and back. And I believe,

when I look at dragonflies,
        that they are the ones who bring the evening down.

I believe they are the ones
            who lift the morning's head.

I recognize them.   Recognize the hope in them. The promising.

Look at us taking all the light in the world away, they tell me.
            And look at us. Look. Bringing every bright drop back.

Acknowledgments

2020 and 2021 were the hardest years of my career so far. I started writing this book around the end of 2021. I didn't think it would go anywhere, because nothing I'd written after 2018 had gone anywhere. I sent my agent an email: "It might be really boring? I don't know. Maybe you can tell me what you think." I wasn't trying to be modest or anything. I had run out of faith in myself. Luckily, though, Patricia never ran out of faith in me. Throughout that dark period, my conversations with her were like a light through fog. She helped me turn that first draft into the book you're holding now. Patricia, after almost ten years of working together, your generosity and genius still astound me. Thank you for making this life possible for me.

I'm so grateful to all the people who told me to keep going. My dad, who helped me out financially so that I would have time to write. My mom, who never turns down a cup of tea. Chalk, who got me moving, and Ash, who would call me during lockdown to talk about our childhood. And—of course—Liale. "But what am I going to do with my life?" I would ask him. And he would say, "You're going to write another book." Liale, you have always seen me. I love you and I couldn't live life without you.

Thank you to the whole team at Viking. Meriam: thank you for your gentle guidance, for your enthusiasm and brightness, and, yes, for that life-changing email. I can't wait for what the future holds. Thank you to Aykut Aydoğdu for the most beautiful cover art I have ever seen.

Thank you to Amy for reading an early draft, and to Lindsay, who talked to me every week on Skype and who always reminds me that I am, in fact, a good writer. Thank you to Alejandro Zarazua and Ale Fragoso, whose kindness can be felt across the world. Alejandro, you helped me find a way back to music. Whatever gratitude I can express here doesn't feel like enough. And Anna: thank you for helping me to know myself. This book wouldn't exist without the hours we have spent together.

Thank you to the writers whose work has buoyed and fed me, the writers who have shown me what is possible. Oh, just thank you, books. Books that have lived with me and loved me. And I have to thank Sharon Van Etten for making music and for talking so openly about her journey. I wrote and edited this book listening to *Remind Me Tomorrow* and *We've Been Going About This All Wrong* on repeat. We don't know each other, Sharon, but your voice has carried me.

And then, finally: our daughter was born in September 2023 and immediately set about reinventing the world. Thank you, darling girl, for being our sky and our mountain.

.